THE FLASH CHILDREN

Mabel Esther Allan

The Flash Children

ILLUSTRATED BY GAVIN ROWE

DODD, MEAD & COMPANY   NEW YORK

Library of Congress Cataloging in Publication Data

Allan, Mabel Esther.
  The flash children.

  SUMMARY: Unsure whether they will like their new
home in Cheshire, three children soon become involved
with a visually handicapped schoolmate and the restora-
tion of a British manor house.
  [1. England—Fiction]   I. Rowe, Gavin.   II. Title.
PZ7.A4Fl3   [Fic]   75-11445
ISBN 0-396-07229-1

Contents

Chapter One

The house by the flash

On a hot day in early July the Briggs family said goodbye to Melwardley and took the road North. The road that led from Shropshire into Cheshire, where their new home was to be. And, as she sat in the back of the loaded old car, squashed between Arthur and Megan, Dilys wondered how she was going to bear it. Beside her, Arthur was wondering much the same thing. Megan was just trying not to be sick before the journey had really started.

Megan was only six and she was a bad traveller; also she had been upset by all the tensions coming from the others. Saying goodbye to that familiar, beloved scene had been awful. Arthur was eleven, tall and fair, and Dilys was ten. The two girls were small and dark like their Welsh mother. 'Won't we ever come back?' Dilys asked. They had had their last glimpse of the lovely Breiddens beyond the River Severn, and the road North stretched ahead, crowded with traffic. 'Won't we ever see our friends again?'

'You'll make new friends. Children always do,' said their father, George Briggs, over his shoulder.

'But—' Dilys knew she shouldn't persist. She knew that her mother also minded leaving the gentle country that was

7

within sight of her native Wales. But it was dreadful to see it for the last time . . . worse than she had imagined.

They had had to go. Their father had been head cowman on a great estate, but the estate had been sold, and there was going to be an Army camp there, with houses for officers and a big training ground. Their father had tried to find another good job in the neighbourhood, but nothing had turned up quickly enough, and the job in Cheshire was well paid. He would be in charge of a pedigree herd of British Friesians; a very famous herd, he had explained. And the house that went with the job was a good one.

Their mother had seen the house. She had been up there to look it over. She had come back rather subdued and uncommunicative, but she had agreed with her husband that it was a good house. Only . . .

The children didn't know what that 'only' had meant. There had been talk of a flash; a strange word. A flash, it turned out, was a lake; one that had formed in salt country, where the land had subsided. There were many flashes in Cheshire around Northwich, Middlewich and other towns. A lake sounded all right, but it wouldn't make up for losing all their friends, and having to go to a new school for the two and a half weeks that remained before summer holidays.

'I feel sick!' Megan wailed. Her wail rose above the frantic mewing of Red, their ginger cat, who hated being shut up in a basket.

'Oh, no!' groaned Mr Briggs. They were passing through

8

a large village of unattractive brick houses. 'Meg, dear, I can't stop here.' He frowned at the road ahead, his sun-tanned face anxious and worried. He was fair and big, and generally very good-tempered and kind.

Mrs Briggs twisted around as well as she could, for she was holding the cat basket on her knee, and there were things on her feet.

'Oh, yes, I'm afraid so!' she said, in her lilting voice, when she saw her younger daughter's green face.

'Well, don't be sick on me,' Dilys grumbled. That would only make everything ten times worse. *She* was never sick . . . hated it. Oh, Melwardley, lost forever! And her best friend, Joan, daughter of the estate manager. Joan and her family were moving to Herefordshire.

They left the village behind, and, by great good luck, there was a lay-by. The old car swept in and stopped, and Megan scrabbled frantically at the door handle. Tumbling out just in time, she was sick in the piled gravel against a bank. Dilys looked the other way, but Arthur, like his father by nature, as well as in looks, got out and held her.

It didn't seem a good beginning to their new lives, but was, after all, to be expected. Megan never had been able to travel far by car, though she was all right in the school bus.

Behind them there was a loud hooting sound, and it was the furniture van. The driver pulled in and waited. The arrangement was that he should follow, as he didn't know the way to Flash Cottage.

9

Megan and Arthur got into the car again, and Mrs Briggs managed to find some barley sugar. Megan sucked and said she felt better. So the journey into Cheshire went on, and wasn't really so very far.

'Cheshire cheese and Cheshire cats,' said Arthur. 'Red will be a Cheshire cat now, I suppose. Is it near here, Dad? It doesn't look like country.'

It didn't; at least, not like the lovely, curving country they had left, with glimpses of blue hills and winding river. There were flat fields, some pasture and some where oats and wheat were ripening, with sometimes an old black and white cottage. But not far away there was industry; huge buildings and cooling towers.

'North Midland Chemicals,' said Mr Briggs. 'We're nearly there now.'

They turned at a cross roads on to quite a narrow road. Soon there was a very large farmhouse, red brick and hideous, and a big group of farm buildings. In fields on either side of the road black and white Friesian cows grazed peacefully in the July heat.

'The Salthouse Flash herd,' said Mr Briggs, his worried expression lightening. 'Fine, aren't they? Wonderful beasts.'

The children hardly glanced at them. They were too hot, uncomfortable and unhappy. The road narrowed and grew rougher, and Arthur gave a cry of surprise. For the 'flash' lay ahead; a big sheet of water, whipped into waves by the brisk, hot wind. The nearest shore was thickly edged with reeds, and there were ducks and other water fowl. Across the middle of the flash the road continued as a causeway.

'Are we going over?' Dilys asked.

'Yes. That's our house.' Her father gave a brief wave, then concentrated on the way ahead. The causeway was quite wide, but unfenced.

They gazed ahead in disbelief. Beyond the flash there was not much land, just a narrow strip of green, then an enormously high railway embankment. Against the embankment, to the right of the road, was a fairly modern brick house, stark and ugly. Flash Cottage it was called . . . but it wasn't a cottage. It was the kind of house that is easy to draw, with plain windows in rows, and a red-painted front door in the middle. The roof was of slates and chimneys stuck up like a donkey's ears.

Their house on the Melwardley estate had been built partly of timber, and partly of rosy bricks nearly three hundred years old. Clematis had grown over the porch, and a lovely creeper over one wall. They had left a large garden full of roses, delphiniums and poppies, but, as the car stopped and they scrambled out, Dilys saw that the small garden behind a red-painted gate held nothing but overgrown grass and some straggling nasturtiums.

Dwarfed by the great embankment and the silent house, the three children stood in a group. No one spoke until Mr Briggs said: 'Jump to it, Dilys! Take the cat from your mother. Here comes the furniture van.'

At that moment, with a high, echoing hoot, a long blue

train passed at a great speed over their heads. Its passing seemed to break the spell, and Arthur looked up, suddenly pleased.

'Gosh!' he cried, when the great express had gone. 'What a super train! Electric . . . I can see the overheads.'

'That,' said his father, sounding more himself, 'must be one of the Manchester–London expresses. They travel at a hundred miles an hour, or maybe even more.'

In their part of Shropshire there had been no trains. Dilys didn't much like the idea of having such fast ones roaring past over their heads, but she could see that Arthur was interested.

The next two hours were busy and bewildering. The children helped where they could, though Megan spent most of the time crouching among the nasturtiums with Red. Red was a ginger male, seven months old. A young cat of great character and energy, but now he was scared

and puzzled. He delicately ate a bit of rabbit, brought specially as comfort, then lay with his tail furled and his eyes wild and watchful.

Arthur agreed to take a bedroom at the back. It was quite a nice big room, with fresh yellow paint, but the only view was of the rising embankment, covered on its lower slopes by elderberry bushes.

'I don't mind,' he said to Dilys, when she carried in a box that contained some of his books and old games and puzzles. 'If I look right up I can see the trains.'

'And hear them without looking up,' said Dilys. They eyed each other, understanding just how each felt. It was all so strange, so alien. And promised to be so lonely.

Dilys went back into the room she and Megan were to share. The old blue carpet was already down, and her mother was standing on a step-ladder to fix the new blue curtains. Beyond her slender, poised figure the Cheshire

13

scene shimmered in the heat. Flash, distant farm and buildings, and the great, grim sweep of North Midland Chemicals nearly two miles away.

The removal men came in with Megan's bed, then with Dilys's. Dilys went out, without speaking, and joined Megan among the nasturtiums. Megan's face was pink again, but she looked sober.

'Are we going to stay here forever, Dilly?' she asked.

'I suppose so; for years, anyway. Don't you like it?' Dilys waited for the answer with some curiosity.

'Too much ugly,' said Megan, and dropped an orange flower on Red's nearly orange head.

'But the flash isn't ugly,' said Dilys. 'I wonder if there's a boat on it. That would be nice.' It was all she could think of that might be enjoyable. She and Arthur could both row. They had learned on the Severn, when the water was low and quiet in summer.

When the men went it was evening, and the golden sun had moved around until it was shining into the front windows, and striking back dazzlingly from the flash. Mrs Briggs was in the kitchen, preparing a meal. It was a good kitchen, with an electric stove and a refrigerator, but was rather dark because of the embankment.

With their furniture more or less in place the house looked less bleak and strange, but still it wasn't home. It was a long time since the children had been so silent. Their father wandered around, doing odd jobs, glancing at them occasionally. Dilys knew they ought to say something, to try to look happier, but it was difficult . . . impossible.

But the food tasted good, and they all felt better after the meal.

'It's Saturday tomorrow,' said Mrs Briggs. 'So you can start exploring. But all you children must be very careful.' She said 'fery' and her voice always rose at the end of a sentence. 'The flash is what I am worrying about. That open causeway . . .'

'We didn't fall into the Severn. We won't fall into the flash, Mother,' Arthur said. And then: 'Where's school?'

'In Southwich. You remember the cross roads where we turned? You catch the school bus there on Monday morning. I've seen the school. It's a fairly new one, and children go there from all over this countryside.'

15

Mr Briggs ate his meal, then said he was going over to Salthouse Flash Farm to see his new boss, Colonel Melling. He walked away into the golden evening, and they watched his figure growing smaller as he crossed the causeway. Mrs Briggs went back to the kitchen, but told the children not to help with the dishes. Just for once they could go out without helping.

They went, followed by Red, but Red didn't venture beyond the gate.

'The road goes on under the railway,' Arthur said, and they walked into the cool, shadowy tunnel under the embankment. Ahead, narrow and rough, the lane went on between high banks, leading into unknown country.

'I hate it!' said Dilys. 'I'll never like it. But we mustn't let Dad and Mother know. I see that now. Meg, you'll be good, won't you? You won't say anything? Not about too much ugly and that?'

Megan shook her head. 'I won't say.'

The two elder ones looked at each other over her head.

'We'll get to know it,' Arthur said. 'Won't we? There must be other kids.'

They walked slowly northward over the causeway. At the eastern end of the flash, close to the water, they could see a cottage. It was a real cottage, half-timbered, with an uneven roofline. It looked very old and they wondered if it was empty. There seemed to be no curtains at the windows, but it was too far off for them to be sure.

'It's nice to see something old, when everything looks so

new. Well, sort of half-new,' said Dilys. She frowned at the dancing water and the wind whipped her hair into her eyes. 'I wish I knew what kind of things we'll do. Could we fish?'

Arthur frowned, too.

'Won't it be salty? You remember Dad said at tea that once there were brine pumps, taking out the salt.'

'Perhaps we could learn about birds. I don't believe there are any flowers here.' In Melwardley there had been wild flowers everywhere, and she and Arthur had made a big collection. It had been much praised at school. 'We could add nasturtiums to our collection,' Dilys added glumly.

'Not wild.'

'I *know*. I was being sarcastic. And what'll Meg do?'

'No one to play with,' said Megan sadly. Joan's younger sister, Mary, had been her best friend. 'And no garden. I had to leave my sweet peas.'

'Only that beastly patch,' grumbled Arthur. They all three loved gardening and knew a good deal about it.

'There'll be the farm,' Dilys pointed out. 'We always helped at Melwardley. But it's not like the estate, is it?'

'Mostly the herd, and some general farming,' said her brother. 'Two hundred acres.' Melwardley estate had been nearly two thousand acres, with fields and woods rolling down to the River Severn.

They were almost over the causeway, and suddenly Dilys pointed, crying: 'Look! A boy and girl. Over there in the reeds.'

Chapter Two

The school bus

The boy and girl, who looked around their own ages, were crouching in the reeds. All they could see of them were their heads, with brown hair, and the tops of a blue and a white sweater. Then a bare arm flashed upward, something hurtled through the air, and there was consternation among a group of black and white ducks. They streaked away, flapping and quacking, and a laugh came on the wind. Another stone was thrown after the birds.

'Stop that!' Arthur shouted. 'Stop it at once!'

Dilys pulled his arm anxiously. 'Don't quarrel. Don't make them mad.'

'I don't care,' her brother said fiercely. 'That first stone was meant to hurt the birds.'

'But we need friends . . .'

The two children were ploughing their way out of the reeds. Below the sleeveless sweaters were two pairs of grey shorts and long brown legs. As the Briggs trio reached the end of the causeway, the strangers leaped onto the road.

'Mind your own business,' said the boy aggressively.

'We won't if you do things like that.'

18

'You must be the Briggs kids,' remarked the girl. She was plain, with pale blue eyes, and a sulky expression. 'We saw you pass in the car earlier, and the furniture van.'

'Yes,' said Arthur. 'Arthur, Dilys and Megan.' And, in a spirit of sheer mischief, he added something in Welsh. The strangers took two steps backward, looking astonished.

'French,' said the boy. 'They're foreigners. But Dad said . . .'

'Don't be silly, Dan! You *are* silly! That was Welsh. Only of course you're too stupid to know,' said his sister.

'You shut up! I'm not silly, or stupid.'

'Dad *said* Mrs Briggs was Welsh, and Dilys and Megan are Welsh names. Perhaps Arthur is, too,' she added doubtfully.

'King Arthur still lies sleeping under a hill,' Arthur said solemnly. 'With his knights. Do you quarrel with *each other*?'

'Sometimes,' admitted the girl. 'There's nothing to do here. When we have money we take the bus into Southwich. There's more there. Colonel Melling won't have us around the buildings. Dan teases the animals.'

'So do *you*. It was you who threw a clod of earth at Salthouse Samantha.'

Megan was staring in round-eyed surprise and disapproval. Arthur and Dilys looked at each other, and Dilys shrugged. They were relieved to see their father striding toward them. Ignoring the two strange children, they all ran forward.

19

'Dad! Are you going back now?' Dilys couldn't say 'home' yet.

'Yes, I am.' When they were out on the causeway Mr Briggs asked: 'What was going on? Those were the Brown kids; Dan and Edith. Their father works for Colonel Melling. They live in that little house before you get to the farm.'

'They were throwing stones at the birds. They . . . I didn't like them,' said Dilys.

'That's a pity,' their father said. 'They're the nearest children.'

'*I* didn't like them a bit,' Megan said.

'I'm afraid the Colonel doesn't either,' he said. 'But they can't be as bad as all that. Their mother died about a year ago, and they're looked after by an aunt. She can't manage them, though of course that's in confidence.' He looked at the raised faces of his children, brightly lit by the brilliance of the lowering sun. Ahead the embankment was half in shadow, and a goods train rumbled slowly above the roof of their new home. 'Look here, you're all sensible. Don't condemn Dan and Edith before you really know them.'

The water slapped, the reeds rustled, the goods train went off into the golden distance.

'Arthur was a bit too clever,' said Dilys. 'Talked Welsh, and about King Arthur.'

'Well,' said Arthur defensively. 'I couldn't help it.'

'Anyway,' Mr Briggs said, as they reached their new home, 'Colonel Melling wants to meet you in the morning.

You're to come up to the house – Salthouse Flash Farm –
at ten o'clock.'

'Gosh! To be looked over?'

'Something like that,' Mr Briggs agreed ruefully. He had
the deepest misgivings over whether he had done the right
thing in bringing his family into this rather harsh countryside.

'Washed behind the ears?' asked Dilys, giggling. Half-
scared.

'Of course. But he's quite a nice man, really. He left the
Army and bought this place, and the herd is famous. His
sons are grown up, and the younger one helps him.'

'Must *I* meet him, washed behind the ears?' asked
Megan.

'Yes, you must. Ten o'clock, remember.'

They had milk and biscuits and went to bed. Megan fell
asleep almost at once, but Dilys lay wakefully, lonely and
unhappy. After a time she slipped out of bed and went to
the window. It was almost dark, but she could still dimly
see the great cooling towers and the glow of a furnace.
Behind her, out of sight, an express sped past. The embankment curved a little, and after a while she could see the
long, lighted train speeding toward Manchester.

'Too much ugly.' Her heart yearned for the place they
had left, where dusk came so softly over the unspoilt
countryside. Yet it was going to be spoilt and this was their
new place . . . their new life. School bus on Monday, and

everything strange, unfamiliar. But it had to be faced.

Arthur, at his window, saw the London express pass overhead. He could even see people sitting in the dining car. He thought of Colonel Melling, who didn't welcome children, and of Dan and Edith Brown. Edith . . . funny name! Birds . . . a salt flash . . . no flowers. He could perhaps collect engine numbers, and learn about trains. Finally he went back to bed and slept deeply until he heard the house stirring at five-thirty. Milking was at six, and his father had to be there to supervise. Salthouse Samantha, he thought sleepily. At Melwardley there had been a mixed herd of Shorthorns, Herefords, Friesians, a few Ayrshires. Nothing very special. This was a great and famous herd, every calf entered in the herd book.

'I shan't be a farmer, or a farm worker, or anything like that,' Arthur told himself. 'I shall be clever . . . really clever. Go to college, do something interesting. Travel.'

He knew, really, that farmers nowadays had to be clever, and that they often went to special colleges. But there were other things to do, and trains carried people far away. One went rushing past on its way to London as he turned over for another hour's sleep.

The week-end passed slowly. The three children went to meet Colonel Melling and his wife. They were not so very old, and quite nice in a stiff kind of way. The farmhouse was huge, but terribly ugly, and all the buildings were modern, with nothing in the least tumble-down and romantic.

They walked through the shippons (as cowsheds were called in Cheshire) with Colonel Melling, and were shown the milking machines. They were introduced to the latest calves, charming black and white creatures with impressive names. Salthouse Selina, Salthouse Silver, Salthouse Susanna, and a little bull, Salthouse Sylvester.

He showed them some of the farm machinery . . . everything as modern as possible. And then walked them over a few fields. Wherever they walked they could see the great railway embankment, and the upthrusting towers of North Midland Chemicals. Every hedge was cut back so that there was no chance of wild flowers, and every fence and gate was in perfect order. It was frightfully dull, and the children grew more homesick for Melwardley every minute.

In the afternoon they went into Southwich with their mother to do some shopping, and that was better. It was an old 'salt town', with some black and white buildings, and two huge ancient crosses in the main square. They walked to the other side of the little town to look at their school, which was large and glassy and had bright blue doors. Across the playground was another building, and that was where Megan would go, so they wouldn't be far apart.

Arthur and Dilys tried to talk as if everything was all right, and their mother was rather too bright, but they all fell silent going back in the bus to the cross roads. At the cross roads there was a signpost and the one that pointed down their lane said: 'Salthouse Flash ½ mile.

23

Unmade road to Nether Pelverden.' And signs to show the railway bridge, and unfit for traffic beyond it.

'What's Nether Pelverden?' asked Arthur.

'I think it's a very small village about three miles away,' Mrs Briggs said.

As they crossed the flash the sun went in, and the heavy clouds that had been piling up grew darker. Thunder was rumbling as they approached the railway embankment. Soon the rain was pouring down and thunder crashed over-head. A strange wind had sprung up, and waves broke over the causeway.

It rained all Sunday. They helped in the house, watched television, and thought that the day would never end. Rain had never seemed to matter in Shropshire; they'd have been around the estate in raincoats and rubber boots, or playing in the barns.

'What are we going to *do* here?' Dilys groaned, as she and Arthur met outside the bathroom on their way to bed. 'We'll get like those two Brown kids soon and start throwing stones at the ducks.'

They were glad when it was time to set off to catch the school bus, though Megan, scared and reluctant, dragged behind. They met Dan and Edith and went on together to the corner. The Browns were neither friendly nor un-friendly, just blank. They looked sleepy and Dan was still eating his breakfast, a bacon sandwich.

'Half the time we miss the bus,' Edith said.

When the bus came it was already fairly full with noisy

boys and girls, and the driver said to Arthur, Dilys and Megan: 'You're the flash children? Right? I was told there'd be three new ones.'

The flash children! That was what they were now. They belonged to this harsh countryside. Dilys sat with Megan on her knee and listened to the rumpus. In Shropshire, it seemed to her, everything had been perfect. Even the children had behaved better, and they had all had such lilting voices.

But school wasn't bad. Arthur's teacher was a Miss Frayne, and Dilys's class had a man, very young and rather nice, called Mr Dell. Dilys quite liked a girl called Lally Reach, but she lived on a farm three miles from Salthouse Flash, and would be no use as an out of school companion.

There were thirty boys and girls in the class, and near her was a boy with longish dark hair, and he wore very thick glasses. He worked with his nose nearly on his book,

and looked hunched and withdrawn, but she noticed that he got high marks for a story the members of the class had had to write last week. His name was Brian Pelverden, and that was odd; the same as the village. During playtime he wandered alone in the playground.

Dilys looked for Brian in the school bus going home, but he was not there. She told Arthur about him, and Arthur said: 'He must be that half-blind kid.'

'Half-blind?' Dilys asked, in horror.

'Well, partially sighted, they call it. I heard some of the boys in my class talking about him. He's only been in school about a month. He's new to the neighbourhood, too. There was a row last week because they teased him.'

'Beasts!' cried Dilys. 'He looks interesting. He's quite nice looking, except for those glasses and a sort of hunch. How did you get on, Meggie?'

'I am clever,' said Megan. 'My teacher said so. Some of the children in my class can't *read*. I told her I can read anything.' Megan could, pretty nearly. She had never been taught to read, but had read something out of the newspaper when she was just five.

It was a very wet week. The oats and wheat were soaking in the fields, and the road was full of puddles. They could not go out in the evenings, and the dreary countryside brooded in the mist. They could not even go out during playtime most days, but on Friday the sun began to shine, and out they all went. Some of the older children began to torment Brian Pelverden.

'Owl!' they shouted at him. 'Goggles! Can't even see the blackboard.'

Dan and Edith were the worst. Brian merely said: 'You shut up!' and began to walk away, but they followed him.

Dilys happened to be with Arthur just then, and she cried:

'We must stop them! *Please*, Arthur!'

'I should think so,' agreed Arthur, squaring his shoulders and looking very like his father.

They both raced after the taunting crowd and scattered them with the force of their arrival. Arthur hit a boy called Bobby and just missed Dan's ear. Dilys shouted: 'You are all horrible! *Cruel!* I'm ashamed of you. Edith, *stop* it!' She seized Edith by the back of her dress and shook her until her teeth rattled. 'You're disgusting!' she cried. 'You deserve to be struck *deaf* and see how you like it.'

Edith had the grace to look ashamed. The others, after deciding not to fight Arthur, began to slink away. They had already been in one row over teasing Brian.

'I didn't mean to be,' Edith muttered.

Brian had stopped and was kicking the asphalt with his worn shoes. He didn't look friendly, or grateful, but Dilys went up to him. She did, in a strange way, very much like the look of him, even if he wasn't friendly.

'Where do you live?' she asked. 'We don't see you on the school bus.'

'Oh, I get the other bus along the road to Nether Pelverden and Snaith,' Brian said. She noticed that he had a low, attractive voice, and his eyes were large and rather beautiful behind the awful glasses.

Then the bell rang and they went in. Brian walked confidently enough up the steps and into the classroom, so he could see to some extent. Dilys wondered what it must be like to have something wrong with you. But there was nothing wrong with his *brain*, or with his voice. The last lesson was singing and she heard his voice rising, very clear and sweet.

'I wish I had the chance to ask him,' she said to Arthur, when they were on the bus, 'why his name is the same as the village. Though you said he was new to the neighbourhood.'

It seemed a small mystery.

Chapter Three

Dilys's picture

They had been living by Salthouse Flash for a week. But it seemed more like months since they had said goodbye to Melwardley and all their friends and interests. Yet all three children missed that lost, gentler place all the time. They knew that their mother missed it, too, though they never heard her say one word of complaint. But her brow was often creased and she sang the most melancholy Welsh songs while she cooked or sewed. That was a sure sign, Dilys thought.

Their father said he liked Salthouse Flash Farm, and the herd was wonderful. ('It's all right if your life is *cows!*' Arthur muttered.) But he certainly had some idea that all was not well with his family, for he often gave them searching looks.

Only Red seemed quite happy. He had settled down; he knew where they all slept, and generally chose Dilys's bed. This wasn't really allowed, for he had his own basket in the kitchen. But Mrs Briggs ignored the happening. Red was growing into a strong and adventurous cat, and he liked to explore. He enjoyed hiding among the reeds, but

29

was terrified of the dark tunnel under the railway. Every time a train passed overhead he looked up with staring eyes.

'It's just as well,' said Arthur, Friday teatime. 'I was scared he'd climb the embankment. Though it *is* very high and steep.'

Mrs Briggs had met Miss Brown, Dan and Edith's aunt. And Miss Brown had suggested that she join the Women's Institute at Milton, the nearest village, a mile beyond the cross roads.

'She's a very nice woman, really,' she said. 'She gave up quite a good job in Southwich to come and look after her brother and the children. But I don't think she knows the first thing about boys and girls.'

'A job?' asked Dilys, who had thought the aunt must be old. They had not seen her yet.

'Yes. She worked in Barlow's, where they sell radios and television sets. Those children lead her a very great dance, I'm afraid. They won't get up in the mornings, and are always in trouble with Colonel Melling.'

Dilys thought of Edith jeering at Brian, then looking ashamed. She didn't like either Dan or Edith, but she was a bit sorry for them.

'Are you going to be friends with them?' asked Mr Briggs, and Arthur answered: 'I shouldn't think so'.

Saturday morning it was very hot again, but cloudy. They did their jobs, then Arthur and Dilys went out. They asked Megan if she wanted to go, but she was working in her 'garden'. She had been given a patch in a corner and told she could do what she liked with it. There wasn't much she *could* do, but she was starting to dig and rake it, and was going to make a border of little stones and transplant some nasturtiums. As Megan had 'green fingers' they would probably grow. But it was a sad sight to see her there.

Arthur and Dilys went under the railway bridge and walked along the lane. The surface was rutted and full of puddles still, but it was much more like the country. The banks were high and overgrown, and there were golden fields of oats and wheat, and a little wood. In the distance the land rose to the semblance of a small hill, and they could see a farmhouse just on the rise, about a mile away.

They went slowly, looking for flowers and insects on the banks. Birds sang, and there was a warm, steamy smell of grass and earth.

'This is better,' said Dilys. 'Away from those awful cooling towers. They look so menacing . . . so ugly.'

But they could still hear the trains rumbling to and from Manchester.

After nearly a mile they came to a branching of the ways. The lane they were on went ahead, climbing a little, and clearly passed the farm. But there was another narrower lane, little more than a path, on the left . . . a real green road, deep and secret. Dilys looked at it with the first real feeling of happiness for a long time. The little green road went down, and there was the distant sound of running water.

At that very moment black clouds they hadn't noticed covered the sun and there was a loud rumble of thunder. Dilys didn't like thunder, though now she was ten, she tried to keep the fact to herself.

Big raindrops began to fall, and in a way she was relieved, though the lane drew her strongly.

'We'll get soaked!' she cried. 'Better go back.'

'Should have brought our raincoats,' said Arthur.

'But it was so *hot*. It's still hot.'

'Let's not bother about getting wet, then,' Arthur suggested, eyeing his sister with amusement. He knew she hated thunder. And, at that moment, there was a louder clap. Dilys began to run back toward the railway bridge and home, and he followed, laughing.

The deluge overtook them before they had gone half a mile, and the mud was slippery. They ran on, soaked to the skin, and hurled themselves under the dark, echoing bridge to find Dan and Edith sheltering there.

'We were this side of the flash,' Dan explained, 'and Edith's scared of thunder. She wouldn't cross the causeway. Where've you been?'

'Exploring,' Dilys gasped, squeezing out her wet hair. 'Got nearly to the farm. Do you often go that way?'

'We did,' said Dan. 'We'd sooner go to Southwich, but sometimes we went that way. Only we can't now.'

'Very mysterious, aren't you?' mocked Arthur. 'Why?'

'We-ell, it's that awful farmer, Mr Lowe,' Edith said. She cowered back from a vivid flash of lightning. 'He said he'd kill us if he saw us anywhere near his land. And we thought he meant it, so we haven't dared.'

'But why?' Arthur demanded. 'What did you do to make him so mad?'

'Well, we . . . he's never liked us,' Dan admitted. 'Once we stole some plums, just for fun. And then we left a gate open and all his young stock got out. And a heifer

33

wandered right down to the flash and got stuck in the mud. He knew it was us, and he said . . . He has a real temper,' he ended defensively.

Children of a great estate, of a farm worker, Dilys and Arthur stared at them in surprise and horror.

'But how could you be so silly? You must have known to shut gates.'

'I got stung by a wasp,' said Edith, 'and we just forgot the gate. He said we did it on purpose. So we don't go now, and I liked it. There's a stream, and a ruined mill, and that old manor house place. We'd been there, that day. All empty and starting to fall down. It was fun breaking windows.'

'Manor house? How do you mean?' Dilys was beginning, when the storm increased in fury. 'I'm going *home*!' she yelled, and ran out into the downpour, shading her eyes from the glare. 'Come, if you like.' Arthur followed her, just as she slipped and fell. She was up again in a moment and pushing open the gate of their home. They hurled themselves indoors. The Browns did not follow, and, since there was a fuss while they got dried and Dilys's cut and muddy knee was bathed, they didn't even remember them until the storm had passed.

'Some time,' said Dilys later, to Arthur, 'we must go and look for that ruined mill and manor house. I never dreamed there was anything interesting here.'

But her knee hurt, and the lane under the bridge was a

sea of glutinous brown mud. So, in the hot sun of late afternoon, all three children walked slowly along the top of the flash toward the distant old cottage. The path was narrow and slippery, close against the reeds, and, after a short time, the railway embankment hemmed them in. Suddenly Arthur cried:

'Look! An old boat!' He pointed, and the other two saw it lying against the reeds, tied to a low post.

'It isn't that old,' said Dilys, after a careful inspection. 'There are oars, and the only water in it must be rain water. I should think it's safe.'

'Oh, please let's go out in the boat,' begged Megan. She had been so quiet lately that both wanted to please her. Besides, it would be good to row on the flash, and surely quite safe.

'It must belong to someone,' said Arthur. 'But we'll do no harm. Jump in!' He untied the rope, then took one oar, while Dilys took the other. They pushed themselves out on to the flash, but they had scarcely rowed three yards when there was a shout. A man was coming along the path from the direction of the old cottage.

'Oh, dear! It's his!' Dilys groaned, and they began to move the boat back into the gap in the reeds. 'We're terribly sorry!' she called, as the man approached.

He was tall, and he had rather long greying hair and a good-looking, sun-tanned face. His sweater and trousers were very old.

'We only meant to borrow it for a little while,' Dilys went on. 'You see, we have nothing to do, and we *can* row.'

He came to the edge of the flash and looked at them closely. 'You must be the children from Flash Cottage. I didn't see the little girl at first. I thought you were that pair of young devils, Dan and Edith. The sun was in my eyes.'

'No,' said Arthur. 'We're Arthur, Dilys and Megan Briggs.'

'And I'm John Zachary Laurie. I'm an artist, and I'm living in that cottage along there for the summer. Here, let me come out with you for a while. I know where the shallow parts are. You might easily have got stuck.'

He climbed into the boat and took the oars, adding: '*You* can row out in the middle.'

It was lovely on the water, and they soon forgot to be shy. In fact, they were soon telling him all about leaving Shropshire, and how they hated living by Salthouse Flash. Not much to do, and no friends, and it was all so ugly. The artist listened, seeming very interested.

'It isn't really ugly,' he said, after a while. 'It has something. Dramatic effects, you know, and design. I paint it all the time.'

'Real pictures?' asked Megan.

'Yes. I'll show them to you, if you like, and you can have some lemonade.' He was taking the boat back, and, as he tied it up, they eyed each other. They had been told so often not to talk to strangers; not to go with strangers. Mr Laurie seemed to know what they were thinking.

'It's all right, honest. I know Colonel Melling, and I'll go home with you in a few minutes and meet your parents. I've been meaning to call and say hello.'

They went with him along the path, and the cottage turned out to be as old as Dilys had thought. It had a charming, tangly little garden, and they all sat on a bench outside the front door while Mr Laurie fetched lemonade. Then Dilys, more curious than the others, ventured into the small front room and found it crammed with paintings,

37

some very small, and some large. They were hanging on the old walls, between the thick oak beams, and even propped against what furniture there was. And each one showed some aspect of that countryside.

They were not in the least like any pictures Dilys had seen before. At school, in Shropshire, there had been a series of flower paintings, and they had two at home . . . a bluebell wood, and a pretty harbour scene. Mr Laurie's pictures seemed composed of angles and they were mostly painted in greys and browns, with sudden dashes of red or yellow. Yet she could *see* that countryside. There was the flash, with even the reeds painted in angular shapes, and the sharp angle of the causeway, with two funny sticklike figures walking over. Whenever there were people they were sticklike, but it was Dan and Edith going over the causeway.

'Dan and Edith!' she said, and Mr Laurie laughed behind her.

Dilys moved slowly around. She felt a little embarrassed, for they were such odd pictures . . . sort of childish. There was Salthouse Flash Farm, just suggested, but recognisable. Very ugly. And the cooling towers across the flash and fields, against a stark yellow sunset sky.

After a few minutes she began to be enchanted, as if she were seeing that landscape for the first time. And then she came to a small painting propped against an old wooden chair. It showed their own grim little house, with the arch of the railway bridge, and the embankment rising behind like a thundercloud with spikes. But the spikes and lines were the overhead electric wires.

'Why did you paint *our house?*' she asked.

'The angles were interesting,' the artist said. 'I know you hate that house, but, if you try, you'll see more than you have been doing. You may have that picture, if you like.'

Dilys nodded, and he lifted it up and put it in her arms. It was boldly signed in the right-hand corner 'John Z. Laurie'.

By then Arthur and Megan were inside, too.

'Too much ugly,' Megan murmured, and Dilys kicked her foot. But John Z. Laurie had heard.

'You have to learn to look,' he said. Then he laughed, gave Megan some chocolate, and began to walk with them back along the path. 'Most of the pictures are to be packed up this week and sent off to Manchester. That's where I really live.'

Mr Briggs was at the farm for milking, but Mrs Briggs was there and greeted the artist politely. He didn't stay long, and, when he had left, she laughed.

'The poor man! He can't be making much money out of pictures like that. Where are you going to put it, Dilly?'

'Over my bed,' said Dilys. 'I like it.'

Her mother found her a hook and some cord, and the picture hung on the pale yellow wall . . . grim, but compelling. The more Dilys looked at it the more pleasure it gave her. It was very strange.

She took a last look at it before she drew the curtains

against the sunset light and scrambled under the bedclothes. She found that she felt less lost and unhappy, and couldn't quite understand why. Maybe it was because they were beginning to know people. Dan and Edith, of course, but you couldn't call that *know* . . . Mr Laurie . . . and Brian Pelverden at school. Next week she'd try to get to know Brian better.

Then there was the lane under the railway bridge that led into a world that seemed different. Soon they'd go that way again.

Chapter Four

Under the railway bridge

It wasn't easy to get to know Brian Pelverden. He didn't travel on their school bus, and playtime only lasted ten minutes, morning and afternoon. There was school dinner, but Brian was one of the ones who brought a packed lunch and ate it at a separate table. After dinner he usually disappeared, and it was almost the end of the week before she discovered that he sat in the little school library, reading with his nose almost on a book.

Dilys had quickly grown observant over Brian, and she knew he was clever. Mr Dell seemed to know, too, but even he grew impatient sometimes. When Brian dropped his pencil sharpener and couldn't find it, even though it was quite close to him . . . when he knocked things over . . . all kinds of little happenings that made the other boys and girls in the class giggle. Often she wanted to shout: 'You idiots! It's only because he can't *see*!'

Brian remained impassive, never complaining or offering the obvious explanation. He didn't play games, but he was good at dancing. He had a great sense of rhythm. They had country dancing twice a week, and the second time that week Dilys danced with him. Though he was so good, no one else seemed to want to dance with him.

'That was fun,' she said to him, at the end of the class. 'I like dancing with you.' And Brian looked surprised, but not specially pleased.

'Thanks,' he said abruptly.

Dilys talked about him at home, during meals. And her mother said: 'Poor little boy! He ought to be in a special school. I wonder why he isn't?'

Dilys knew about special schools. There had been two children from Melwardley who had gone to one a few miles away. The boy had been very, very stupid and the girl very deaf.

'But, Mother, he's all right. He's the cleverest of the lot. Only the others laugh . . . they're horrible. As if he had three heads, not just can't see very well.'

'The one who is different,' Mr Briggs said. 'It happens with animals, too. He'd be happier in a different kind of school.'

Dilys wasn't sure that Brian would. He seemed to fight pretty hard to be ordinary. The trouble was that he wasn't friendly. If he'd just say quietly: 'I can't see that!' and then be nice to them, the others might learn to accept him as he was.

Thursday dinnertime, when she found him in the library, she asked: 'What are you reading?'

'A book about old houses,' Brian answered. 'The old halls and manor houses of England. You see . . .' And then the bell rang.

When they went home on Friday there was the knowledge that there were only three more days of school. Wednesday afternoon next week the long summer holidays would start. And all three Briggs children were sorry. School gave a pattern to the days. Without it what would they do? During that week Arthur had quarrelled fiercely with Dan Brown, because Dan had deliberately spilled water from a flower vase on the window sill over a treasured drawing. And Edith seemed sulkier than ever; no kind of friend. As for poor Megan, she had made friends in school, but none lived near Flash Cottage.

But at least the countryside seemed more familiar, and Dilys often found herself looking at it with John Z. Laurie's eyes. When they met him on Friday evening she told him so, and he laughed, but looked pleased.

Saturday was fine and hot, and, when they had done their jobs, Dilys suggested: 'Let's go under the railway bridge. Let's find the mill and the manor house. You come too, Meggie.'

'Can she walk that far?' Mrs Briggs asked. She had heard about the narrow green road and what might lie beyond.

'I can walk *miles*,' Megan said, with dignity. 'Me legs are strong.'

'*My* legs.'

'Not your legs. Mine,' said Megan, and tramped off beside them. Red followed them to the railway arch, then retreated, looking over his shoulder as if a fiend were behind. He hadn't come to terms with those roaring trains.

The lane had dried and there was only a little mud. They

came to where the green lane went off to the left without meeting anyone . . . the countryside dreamed under the hot July sun. But, as they turned and started off down the secret way, a man suddenly showed over the hedge on their right. A farmer, clearly, sun-tanned and in his shirt sleeves, with thick grizzled hair. His face was suspicious until he had taken a good look at them, then he smiled.

'Thought you might be those Brown kids,' he explained. 'Are you Mr Lowe?' Arthur squinted upward against the sun. 'No, we're the Briggs children, from Flash Cottage.'

'Oh, yes. Your dad works for Colonel Melling. Know the Browns, do you? Young devils!' he added.

'Yes, we do. They go to our school.'

'They let my young stock out, and I nearly lost a heifer in the flash. I've no love for those two,' he said.

'Edith said she got stung by a wasp and that was why,' Dilys told him. 'They – They have a bad reputation, so you thought they'd done it on purpose.'

'Wasp!' he said grimly. 'They did do it on purpose, mark my words. Sheer mischief!'

Then he disappeared, and once more silence descended on the green place, except for the distant murmur of a stream. Soon they went down into a hollow, and there was the little river, flowing over stones. Near by was a ruined building, with the great mill wheel and grindstones standing up among leaves.

'Could we paddle?' asked Arthur. 'My feet are so hot. It's shallow along there. Deep by the mill.'

44

'Let's go on first,' Dilys said urgently. Manor house . . . could there be? The Browns had taken pleasure in breaking windows.

And it was there, about a hundred yards from the mill; hidden until they were up to the bridge by encroaching old trees. The bridge was a small, ancient one, built of red sandstone, and it spanned a moat. The moat was a startling pale, milky green . . . some kind of moss or weed covering the water. It smelled slightly, but the three children didn't notice. They were all staring at the house.

'Why! The poor, poor house!' Dilys cried. 'So old and beautiful and deserted.'

'It *is* beautiful,' Arthur agreed. 'And frightfully old. Tudor, perhaps.'

The house had a lost, forsaken dignity. It was built on a base of red sandstone, but most of the rest of it was timber and plaster. The black and white patterns filled in two gables, and they could see everywhere the ancient pegs that held the beams in place. Arthur pointed them out. Melwardley Hall had been the same, only larger.

Many of the windows were mullioned – that is, with stone tracery – and a good deal of the glass was broken. Even the lower windows were high above the sandstone base, so Dan and Edith couldn't have climbed in, or even looked in.

They crossed the bridge very quietly. Grass and weeds were growing between the stones, and higher weeds and brambles covered the short space of ground in front of the main door. The door itself was of oak and looked as if it would be immensely thick. Someone had started to carve initials. They could see a faint 'D'.

'Beast!' whispered Dilys.

'Is it the sleeping beauty's palace?' asked Megan, whispering also.

They crept around the side of the house, following the curve of the moat to the left. Then there was an old wall between moat and house, with an old wooden door half-open.

And, beyond, was a walled garden . . . very big, glowing in the sun. It was such a wild tangle of roses, other flowers and high weeds that it might indeed have been part of the sleeping beauty's palace.

'Don't go in!' Dilys whispered, and caught hold of Arthur's shirt from the back.

'Why not? There's no one here?'

Then they all jumped violently when a voice said, 'Hello!' and they spun around to see a small girl behind them.

She had dark hair and a sun-tanned face, and she wore a shabby pink dress. She looked about five.

Megan was delighted and cried, 'Hello!' while the others were merely staring.

'This is our house,' said the little girl. 'You're trespassing. Dad's going to put up a board when he gets time.'

'We're awfully sorry,' said Dilys. 'We thought it was empty. But we weren't doing any harm, you know.' She

spoke as if the child were much older, for the little girl had
sounded so assured.

'Do you live in the house with all the broken windows?'
asked Megan. Then: 'I'm Megan Briggs. Who are you?'

'Mellie Pelverden. Melinda,' said the child. 'We don't
live in the house. In the cottage at the back.'

'Pelverden?' Dilys repeated. Mellie had big dark eyes,
and they had reminded her of someone at once. But this
child didn't look half-blind. 'Have you a brother, then?'

'Brian,' said Mellie. 'He's weeding in the garden. Do you
know him?'

'Yes. He goes to our school. I didn't know he lived *here*.'
It was like a story . . . Dilys could almost believe it to be a
magic house and garden. A place bewitched, and when the
spell was broken it would be whole again. Not desolate
and overgrown and beginning to fall down.

'Come on, then.' And Mellie, beckoning, went ahead into
the garden. They followed, brambles catching at their bare
legs. Mellie led the way down a tangled path to the far
right-hand corner of the garden, and there was Brian Pelverden, in shorts and an old shirt, piling weeds into a
barrow. He heard them coming, and looked up, startled.
He could see well enough to recognise them, for he cried:
'Dilys! And Arthur, isn't it? What are you doing here?'

He didn't sound very pleased, but Dilys and Arthur
began to explain. While they were still talking a man came
up, with a fork over his shoulder. He looked hot and rather
dirty.

47

'Kids from school, Dad,' Brian muttered. 'New to the district, too. They're the flash children. Arthur and Dilys Briggs.'

'And their sister Megan,' Megan said firmly. 'I go to the *other* school. I'm six.'

The man laughed and looked rather pleased.

'A friend for Mellie. That's good! Poor Mellie is lonely. She's starting school in September. Well, you see what a task we have? Do you think we'll ever manage it?'

Arthur and Dilys exchanged glances. They didn't understand at all. Brian said: 'Better explain to them, Dad.'

Mr Pelverden began to talk. 'This is Nether Pelverden Manor, and my family lived here for hundreds of years. The last person to live in the house was my grandfather, and he gradually let it go to rack and ruin. No money to keep it up, and too old to care. When he died he had been living here alone, in a few rooms, but there was a woman in the cottage who looked after him a little. We did try to persuade him to leave, but he wouldn't. My father is dead, and, when the old man died quite recently, the place came to me.'

'It really is like a story,' Dilys murmured.

'Some story, when you think of what we have to do,' Mr Pelverden said grimly. 'We lived in the South. I'm a schoolmaster, but I gave up my job at half-term (with difficulty . . . they weren't pleased) and I have another job in Southwich, starting in September. Hardly any money came with the house, but my wife and I and Brian have set

48

ourselves the task of putting the place in what order we can. So far we haven't done much, for we had to make the cottage habitable first. Fortunately I'm a practical type, and I'll be able to do a lot myself. Put in windows . . . repair the roof of the house.'

'And then live in it?' asked Megan, wide-eyed.

'I hardly think so. But I have a hope,' he said gravely. 'It's a really old house, and, if I could get it scheduled for preservation as an ancient monument, that would be something. We'd get a grant and it would be safe. But I can't have the people concerned seeing the house and garden like this. And the garden alone is going to be hard work.'

Arthur and Dilys had the same idea and started to speak together.

'Couldn't we help? I'd *like* to . . .'

'We could help. We've got nothing to do. And we all love gardening. In Shropshire . . .'

Mr Pelverden looked at them with some amusement. But he seemed pleased.

'You don't know what you're offering. And your parents mightn't like it. Why should you work in the holidays?'

'We'll tell them,' said Arthur. 'They won't mind. They'd be glad. We had a garden in Shropshire, and we always did some work on the estate, too. But there's nothing to do here. We only have a horrid strip of garden, and Colonel Melling won't have children around the farm.'

'It would be splendid!' cried Dilys. 'To help to save the

poor house. It *mustn't* fall down. Honestly, we'd work very hard.'

'What about me?' Megan demanded. 'I can work, too. Things grow for me. And I know which are weeds. All that grass on the bridge, and dandelions on the front steps. Mellie and I could do that.'

'What about it, Brian?' asked Brian's father.

Brian tossed a tangle of bindweed on to the barrow.

'If they want to,' he said ungraciously.

'We really do want to,' Dilys told him. 'It would make all the difference to the summer.'

Chapter Five

Hard work

Mr Pelverden still looked a little doubtful.

'You'd better be shown around before we really decide,' he said. 'Perhaps you'll change your minds when you've seen the magnitude of the task.'

'What's magnitude?' asked Megan.

'It'll be very hard work,' said Mr Pelverden, and laughed. 'Come on, then. You coming, Brian?'

'No, Dad. I'll get on with this,' said Brian.

Mr Pelverden first led Arthur, Dilys and Megan, with Mellie in tow, around the walled garden. In some places it was almost impossible to get through the tangle of briars and overgrown bushes. But there were plenty of flowers... roses, big white and yellow daisies, phlox just opening, and great blue masses of scabious. And on the high, sunny walls peach trees were trained, with bindweed threatening to choke them.

'I've got as far as making a plan of what it should be like,' Mr Pelverden explained. 'This was a herb garden, and some of the plants can be saved. And over there is a lily pond . . . a frightful mess now. And there are raspberries and loganberries, all choked.'

In a far corner of the garden another door led out into a more open space, where there was a yard and a field beyond. At one side of the yard was a small black and white cottage, and a woman with dark hair was pegging clothes on a line. This was Mrs Pelverden, and she seemed delighted when she heard they had offered to help.

'How splendid of you!' she cried. 'And a friend for Mellie, too. Would you like some milk, or lemonade?'

'Lemonade would be lovely, thank you,' said Dilys, and she pegged some clothes on the line, while Mrs Pelverden fetched a large jug of lemonade and some old mugs.

As they drank Mr Pelverden explained that, now, there was no good road to the manor. Once the lane that came down to the mill from the Nether Pelverden side had been much better, but at the moment it was difficult to get the car all the way down. He kept it in a shed a few hundred yards away. The main road was about a mile beyond, and that was where Brian caught the school bus.

'Of course, when I go into Southwich I can take them both,' he said.

Brian . . . Dilys was very curious about him. She wished he had come with them. But when they went back through the garden to see the manor Brian was still working industriously.

They entered the house by a back door. It creaked loudly when pushed back. Inside it was pretty dark, and there was a smell of damp. Something scuttled away, but the children were not scared of rats or mice. Megan was a little scared of the eerie gloom, and still half-expected to find a sleeping beauty.

The kitchen quarters were in a dreadful state. The old stone floors were thick with dirt, and there were piles of boxes and other debris. But the kitchen itself had old oak beams, and a huge wooden table that would seat at least

ten people. The table was very dirty and Dilys longed to scrub it and show up the smooth old wood.

'Could we get lots of hot water?' she asked, and Mr Pelverden nodded.

'We could try lighting the fire and putting on kettles. Look, there are several. They look about fifty years old. There's an electric stove in that corner, but so old I wouldn't trust it. I'm going to have someone in to inspect the wiring. My grandfather was a bit of an eccentric, or felt he couldn't afford electricity bills. I think he used candles at the last. There are bits of candles all over the house. Only a couple of rooms were fully furnished. The solicitors think the other stuff was sold gradually.'

'Perhaps there's something left that *you* could sell,' said Arthur.

'A few things, maybe, but they'll stay with the house. There are some oak settles and chests, and a table to seat twenty in the old dining room.'

'Do you know about it?' Dilys asked. 'Its history, I mean. If Queen Elizabeth slept here or something.'

'It hasn't much history,' Mr Pelverden answered. 'Just a country gentleman's house. Same family for generations. I doubt if anything important happened in this remote place. But it's worth preserving, and that's what I care about, even if we can never contemplate living in it ourselves.'

He led the way along a dark passage from the kitchens, and they came out into a big hall, very high. Dust lay thickly and there was a good deal of rubbish. Spiders' webs hung down from the curving oak staircase.

'I'm going to make a great pile of all the burnable stuff in the field at the back,' said Mr Pelverden.

'When . . . When did your grandfather die?' Dilys whispered, stepping softly, and he laughed at sight of her awed face.

'I don't think there are any ghosts, Dilys. He died a few months ago, but he was in a hospital for nearly a year before that. I came up twice to see him, but he didn't know me. I never saw the house. Then, a few weeks ago, I got word that vandals were starting to do more damage than dust and decay. So I decided to come.'

He stepped back to let Dilys and Arthur go first into what had once been a beautiful room overlooking the bridge and the pale green moat. Rain had come in through the broken windows and it was a damp, sad place.

'Oh, I would love to polish all this lovely panelling,' cried Dilys. 'And wash the floors. Don't you use linseed oil on panelling? I think they did in Melwardley Hall in Shropshire.'

'Hey!' said Mr Pelverden. 'You offered to help in the garden. I think you should all be outdoors in summer, and I'm sure your parents will agree. You're not to come and slave indoors. It'll be a filthy job.'

'But . . .'

'Only occasionally on very wet days, perhaps. Besides, nothing much can be done in here until the windows and roof are repaired. Come upstairs.'

The little ones had gone off to explore on their own. Arthur and Dilys followed Mr Pelverden up the stairs into the dusty, littered bedrooms, then up another flight into smaller rooms, where there were masses of things all covered with dust and cobwebs. Rain had come through the roof and mice scuttled away.

Mr Pelverden stood looking through a little high window in a gable. Arthur and Dilys poked around, wondering if there was any treasure. They jumped when Mr Pelverden said abruptly:

'Look here! You both know Brian. Does he have a bad time in school?'

Arthur and Dilys were embarrassed. Arthur remembered the taunting little mob and was silent. He thought Brian looked all right, and he knew his sister liked him.

Dilys was bolder. 'Yes, he does,' she said. 'I'm in his class. I *know* he can't see very well, and it's not his fault. He's *clever*. But the others are so stupid. They tease him. And . . . And he doesn't help. If he'd just explain, quite naturally, and be more friendly, they'd soon get used to him. I like Brian. I want to be friends.'

'That's good,' said Brian's father. 'Oh, maybe you're too young to understand. He was born that way; with very bad sight. It seems there's nothing much that can be done, but you never know. And at least they seem to think his sight won't get any worse. He's seen endless specialists. I have never wanted him to go to a special school. I want him to try to be normal. But he isn't, of course,' he ended, on a low note. 'Perhaps it's too hard for him. He never talks about it. He gets upset if I mention the subject.'

'He wouldn't like it any better in a special school,' Dilys said, with such confidence that Mr Pelverden looked surprised.

'Did he say so?'

'Oh, of course not. But I think he's proud. He hates to be different, and he *is* clever. Either way it will be . . . Well, hard for him. It's *awful*! But I – I think he'll manage in the end.'

'You are a very perceptive young lady,' said Mr Pelverden, and went abruptly down the steep stairs. Over his shoulder he said: 'If you'll come here this summer I expect you'll soon be real friends. And I'll be grateful.'

They looked for the little ones and suddenly heard laughter from the onetime dining room. It was another room that had windows overlooking the moat. Megan had drawn up an old wooden chair to one end of the great table, and Melinda sat at the other. A vast stretch of dusty wood lay between.

'We're having a banquet,' Megan announced.

'What is the menu?' Mr Pelverden asked. Dilys would have been put off by his tone, for he sounded a little schoolmaster-ish. But that was just his manner, and Megan smiled up at him.

'Venison,' she said firmly.

Mr Pelverden looked quite taken aback, and Dilys herself was surprised.

'How did you hear about venison?' she asked, and Megan wagged her head and laughed.

'It was on television,' she said. 'A banquet in a Scottish castle. And they had venison. So we'll have it here, when the table is all clean and polished. What is it?' she demanded of Mr Pelverden.

'It's the meat of a deer,' he explained, smiling. 'And I don't think you'd like it.'

'I'd sooner have beef burghers,' Melinda said.

'That's not a banquet.' Arthur was laughing, too.

Mr Pelverden was looking from one small girl to the other. But he was seeing, because he had imagination, his ancestors sitting around the great table a long time ago. In the days when they were people of some substance, though never really rich and never important.

'When we've done all we can,' he said abruptly, 'and *if* we get a grant and the house is saved, we'll have a party. We'll have a huge bonfire in the field, and we'll eat in here. Maybe not venison; perhaps only something quite ordinary. But, at the moment, it's only a dream.'

They all went back down the dark, dusty passages, through the kitchens and out into the garden again. Brian was still working, pushing his laden barrow. He hardly looked up.

Dilys felt piqued, wishing he would like them, be more friendly. She knew he didn't want them, and Arthur knew it, too. He caught his sister's eye and grimaced.

'We'll make him be friends,' Dilys whispered. 'We'll make him trust us.'

Mr Pelverden said he would write a note to their parents, and he went into the cottage to do it. The three Briggs children and Melinda sat in the sun on a wooden bench. The two little ones giggled and whispered together.

'Melinda is nice,' Megan announced, as they walked

away through the tangled garden and over the ancient bridge. 'She's very *young*, but we can work, too. I shall bring my little fork and my trowel.'

Dilys and Arthur looked back at the house.

'We've just *got* to save it!' Dilys cried.

It seemed a tremendous task, but, after just three days of school, the holidays stretched ahead. Suddenly they were full of promise . . . made important by a definite purpose.

'What if Dad and Mother won't let us?' Arthur asked.

'They'll be glad,' said Dilys confidently. 'They don't want us to be like Dan and Edith. This is our *work*.'

They forgot about paddling in the stream. They walked back along the green road, along the rutted lane and under the railway bridge. They had been in an enchanted world. It was quite a shock to be back in their own harsh country-side, with the cooling towers of North Midland Chemicals dominating the distant view.

Chapter Six

The walled garden

When they entered the house they found that dinner was almost ready. Their father was home and would be until milking time late in the afternoon. He was reading the paper, and looked up in surprise when he heard the excited chatter.

Mr Briggs had grown used to all three children being rather subdued. The fact had made him unhappy, but he hadn't known what to do about it. Now, it seemed, things were different.

Arthur was waving an envelope under his nose, and Dilys and Megan were speaking in chorus. They were all getting in the way of the dishing up. Mrs Briggs laughed, put down the potato pan, and placed her hands over her ears.

'Goodness me!' she cried. 'What is it all about? Old mill . . . beautiful house falling down . . . work in the garden. What did you find under that railway bridge?'

They calmed down and waited while Mr Briggs read the letter. But he still looked puzzled as he handed it over to his wife. 'He sounds a nice man. A schoolmaster, he says. His children, Brian and Melinda need friends, and you all seem keen on helping to save his old garden. Pelverden? So this is the father of that boy you talked about?'

'Let's sit down to dinner, then they can tell us more,' said Mrs Briggs.

So the story of their morning's adventure was told in detail. Mr and Mrs Briggs were very interested. Both believed in young people having something constructive to do. One of the saddest things about this new environment had been that Colonel Melling wouldn't let them work around the farm.

'Can we go, then?' Arthur asked. 'There's such a lot to do in the garden, and if you saw the house . . . cobwebs everywhere, and maybe treasure in the attics, all dusty. But Mr Pelverden says we must work outdoors, except in bad weather.'

The parents exchanged glances.

'Of course you can go,' said Mrs Briggs.

'And me?' Megan asked, scared of being left out.

'Do you really understand what it's all about, Meggie?' her mother asked. 'It sounds like plenty of hard work. But you could play with the little girl, if it isn't too far to walk.'

'We will play sometimes, but only when we've worked,' Megan cried indignantly. 'Of course I understand. It's to make it all beautiful again, then men will come and give money and it can be better still. I'm going to start on the *dandelions*, and they have awful roots.'

They would all have liked to go back after dinner, but Mr Pelverden had said firmly: 'You can tell Brian on Monday. If it's all right we'll see you on Thursday.'

That was when the holidays started. It seemed a long time to wait.

On Sunday, after morning milking, they took a picnic with them and drove to Delamere Forest. Neither Arthur or Dilys had expected a real forest to be within reach of Flash Cottage.

They played hide and seek in the deepest parts, and while she ran through the dappled shadows, Dilys was really happy. But her thoughts kept on going back to Brian Pelverden and the task that lay before them. Both tasks . . . making friends, and helping to save the old house.

Arthur didn't think of Brian, but he did think often of what they were going to do. He had cleaned his garden tools in readiness. Not that they had really needed cleaning, for, as a true gardener, he always kept them in good order.

That evening, as they all wandered along the top of the flash, they came upon John Z. Laurie. The artist was sitting a few yards from his cottage, painting. It was another picture of the flash, with the farm buildings and cooling towers for a background. But this time the foreground was more important. Several water fowl dominated the scene, much larger than life. Dilys stared at the soft greys and mud browns, the sudden, startling green of the curiously angular rushes. The feathers of the birds were angular, too. He did paint in a strange way, but she had somehow learned a lot since that first time she had seen his work. Her eyes had been busy in every light. They might be childish pictures, but they always showed the scene in a new way.

She wished he might make his fortune with them, but he must be quite poor. Living in that half-furnished old cottage . . . wearing such dreadful clothes.

'Like it?' the artist asked, and gave her a friendly, amused smile.

'Yes, I do,' she said stoutly. 'Mr Laurie, did you ever go under the railway bridge? Have you seen the manor and the mill?'

'Oh, yes,' he said. 'I know that old place. A few weeks ago I did a painting of the manor. Empty, isn't it? And starting to fall down. A pity!'

'It isn't *going* to fall down,' Arthur explained. Then they told him all about Mr Pelverden's plans and how they were going to help.

Later he took them to his cottage and searched around among some canvases. Some had gone, presumably to Manchester. After a moment he held up a picture. Megan gasped and Dilys pressed her arm warningly. One never knew what Megan would say.

The manor house was all angles . . . chimneys and the pattern of the black and white. The bridge was the only curve. Even the brambles and tall weeds were painted like the reeds, with sharp edges. The only real colour was the red-brown of the sandstone, and the stark sweep of pale green that was the moat.

'I envy your Mr Pelverden,' said John Z. Laurie. 'I'd enjoy a task like that.'

When they went back Dana and Edith were in the reeds near the railway bridge, and there was a sudden, frightened yowl. Dan and Edith laughed, and Dan was thrashing the reeds with a long stick. The yowl came again, above the harsh rustling.

'It's Red!' Megan screamed.

Dilys and Arthur ran, stumbling along the narrow path. Dan dropped the stick and both he and Edith turned, as the reeds swished back. But the three Briggs children had seen Red – tail enormous, eyes staring – clinging to a tiny grassy island near the bank.

Arthur punched Dan and Dilys rushed at Edith. Megan, ducking under the flailing arms, pushed through the gap in the reeds. Making tender noises, she rescued Red.

'I say, we didn't mean any harm!' Dan protested. 'But if you want a fight I'm willing.'

'We didn't hurt your cat,' said Edith, scared of Dilys's fury. 'We were only playing with him.'

'I don't want a fight,' Arthur said scornfully. 'Just you keep away, that's all. If you tease Red again . . .'

'Such a fuss about nothing,' grumbled Edith. She and her brother began to walk toward the causeway. 'Everything we do is wrong.'

'They really are *awful!*' cried Dilys, watching the two Browns walking slowly over the causeway. They now seemed to be arguing with each other.

Yet there was something about the pair that made her feel vaguely uncomfortable. They weren't *bad* . . . she was sure of that. And out there on the causeway, with the water slapping on either side, they both looked lonely.

'Some day I think we'll have to do something about them,' Dilys added.

When playtime came on Monday, Dilys determinedly sought out Brian. So far he hadn't even looked in her direction.

'We can come on Thursday,' she said. 'Won't it be fun?'

Brian shrugged and didn't smile.

'Please yourselves,' he said. 'There's plenty to do. I expect you'll soon get tired of it.'

'No, we won't,' Dilys answered. 'We're looking forward to it very much. You'll tell your dad, won't you?'

Brian nodded and walked away.

Every other playtime after that he kept out of Dilys's and Arthur's way. Dilys looked for him in the library, but he wasn't there.

On Wednesday they had their school dinner, and then just stayed for an hour or two. They helped to tidy the class rooms, and heard about classes for next term. By three o'clock they were all rushing out into the playground, on their way home.

The school buses were standing in a different order. Usually the one for Nether Pelverden and Snaith was first in the line, but this time their own was. Dilys saw this from afar, for their driver was leaning against the front.

Then she noticed that Brian was making straight for it. He began to scramble in, and a chorus of voices cried: 'Wrong bus, Four Eyes!'

Dilys clenched her hands, wishing she had been near enough to stop him quietly. This was the kind of mistake she knew, with certainty, that Brian hated making. Probably he couldn't read the indicator, and he hadn't distinguished the different driver.

Brian backed out again, looking hunched, and walked away to the second bus. The others pushed their way in, laughing.

'Owl doesn't even know his own bus!' Dan shouted.

'Next term I'll tackle this lot,' Dilys muttered to Arthur. 'How stupid can you get?'

But her thoughts, as they were driven to the cross roads,

were nearly all directed toward the next day. That was when things would really *start*.

'I hope it's fine tomorrow,' she said anxiously to Arthur, as they went to bed.

'If it isn't we can start on the house,' Arthur said. 'Begin moving things down from the attics, perhaps. I do want to know what's there.' And, as he undressed, he gazed up at the embankment, seeing beyond it, in imagination, to that exciting house. The fast trains passed overhead almost unheeded.

The morning was wonderfully fine, with a thick heat haze. They ate breakfast hurriedly, and even more hurriedly helped to wash the dishes, then made their beds. Dilys and Megan had put on old jeans, to protect their legs against brambles, nettles and thistles.

Mrs Briggs had suggested they take a picnic lunch, so that they wouldn't have the long walk in the middle of the day. Arthur put the food and bottles of lemonade in a little rucksack, and took up his fork, hoe and small, sharp-edged spade. Dilys had the same tools, and Megan carried her little fork and trowel. They all had old gloves, at their father's suggestion.

'No point in tearing your hands to pieces if it's as bad as you say,' he had remarked.

They went under the cool darkness of the railway bridge as if they were entering a secret land. In a way that was how they felt, even Arthur.

They heard the cool rush of the stream as they started

down the green lane. The little valley was faintly moist and misty, but already the hot sun was drying the dew, and the haze would soon be gone.

From the ruined mill they took the little side track through the trees, and in a minute or two there was the house. They stared in delight, then in surprise, for there were men on the roof.

'It's Mr Pelverden and another man!' Arthur cried. 'He said the roof had to be done before anything else in the house. But who'd have believed he'd really be able to do that kind of work? He *must* be a handy type!'

Mr Pelverden had seen them. He shouted down: 'Hello! Glad to see you. The others are in the garden.'

'But how did he get up on that high roof?' Megan demanded.

The answer was plain as soon as they entered the garden. There were two long ladders leaning against the back of the house. On the little, overgrown terrace by the back door there were piles of new wood and a heap of slates.

Melinda came along the tangled paths and the two young ones greeted each other joyously. Brian wasn't in sight at first, then they discovered him over by the pool . . . or rather where the lily pool had once been. He was hacking at a mass of nettles and briars. He glanced up and said: 'Oh, there you are!' After that he simply went on with his work.

Arthur and Dilys felt a little foolish and unwanted, standing there holding their tools. But Mrs Pelverden saved the situation by appearing and taking them to the cottage.

'You'll want to leave your things,' she said. 'Is that your picnic lunch? Goodness, we'd give you food. After all, you're working for us.' She indicated a large plan pinned to the kitchen wall. 'See, this is the map of the garden. How it used to be. But I'm afraid you'll only be cutting down and uprooting for a long time to come. My husband says to watch the herbs . . . there are quite a lot of plants that can be rescued. And leave any flowers that are growing well. That corner was the vegetable patch, and there used to be an asparagus bed. It'll probably be best to clear the paths first. We have made a start on those.'

She laughed when she saw the strong old gloves.

'I can see you really mean business! And your own tools as well. But you'll need clippers and perhaps shears. There are plenty in the shed. Where are the children?'

'We're here!' said Megan, appearing in the doorway. 'We're going to start on the bridge *now*.'

'Well, don't get too hot and tired.'

Megan only laughed, and Melinda ran away to find small tools for herself.

Mrs Pelverden didn't ask where Brian was. Perhaps she understood that her son wasn't very eager for company. So Arthur and Dilys went back to the garden and were soon hard at work. Every so often Dilys raised herself and drew a deep breath as she looked around. The air smelled so hot and sweet, and the old walls glowed in the sun.

She had deliberately chosen the path that led toward the lily pond. After an hour or so she had cleared the worst of the nettles and thistles for a few yards, and was fighting with the brambles. They wrapped themselves around her viciously, so it was perfectly legitimate to call to Brian for help.

He came, dropping his clippers carefully on a stone. His face was dirty, and sweat trickled from under his glasses.

'What's up?' He sounded no more friendly than before.

'Oh, you're wearing gloves! So am I, but this brute is holding me. Good job I put jeans on. Can you cut it away?'

Brian went back for his clippers and released her.

'Thanks!' Dilys shook back her hair. 'Shall I help you to clear the pool?'

'Not room for two,' he said, and returned to the shallow basin. Snubbed, Dilys sighed. But it would be different soon. He couldn't go on like this day after day.

She set to work again in the heart of the overgrown garden. The sun was hot on her back and she was filled with contentment.

Chapter Seven

Capturing Edith

Not far away Arthur was picking up his laden barrow, ready for a trip to the rubbish heap outside the garden. He, too, was happy, and he whistled softly. And around at the front of the house, crouched on all fours, Megan and Melinda fought with the dandelion roots.

'We are clearing the way to the sleeping beauty's palace,' said Megan.

They all had a picnic meal together in the yard by the cottage. Mr Pelverden explained that a retired builder, Ben Smith, was helping him to mend the roof.

'He's getting old,' he said. 'But he's a good worker and knows his job. His father used to be miller here, and they lived in a cottage just beyond the mill . . . gone now.'

'It's very sad the way houses disappear,' Dilys said. 'Even the mill has nearly gone.'

'Well, we'll save this house, I hope,' said Mr Pelverden.

He worked in the garden, too, that afternoon, and Mrs Pelverden joined them for an hour. Mr Pelverden asked Dilys to try and disentangle and cut the bindweed that was strangling the peach trees. She did it carefully and lovingly, delighting to see the trees released. There was some fruit, but not much. The hard golden skins of the peaches were hot against the wall. She wondered if they would ever be eatable.

At four o'clock Mr Pelverden said they had all done enough. He suggested that they went to paddle in the stream.

'But keep where it's shallow,' he warned. 'It's deep by the mill. Watch the little ones, won't you?'

Brian went with them, rather to Dilys's surprise. But he didn't say much and soon he had wandered away alone, the rippling water swirling around his calves. He went slowly and cautiously, as if afraid he wouldn't see the deep places.

'Isn't it heaven?' Dilys asked Arthur.

'Nearly as nice as boating on the Severn,' Arthur answered. They stood together in the dappled shadows cast by willows and alders. A short distance away the remains of the mill wheel and the great grindstones made strange shapes in the green-gold light.

At five o'clock they were on their way up the green lane, walking slowly and rather tiredly. Their faces were tingling after the day in the hot sun, and they were so ravenously hungry that, when the railway bridge came in sight, they made a sudden spurt.

'There's so much to *do*,' Arthur said. 'You feel as if you need six pairs of hands. Do you think we'll ever really make an impression?'

'Don't forget we have weeks,' Dilys answered.

Megan trailed a little way behind. She must be very tired. Dilys waited and took her hot hand.

'Did you enjoy it, Meggie? Do you like working there?'

'Yes.' Megan nodded. 'But there are *so* many dandelions, and the grass between the stones is *awful*. Mellie and I talked all the time.'

'I bet you did,' Arthur said, and laughed. The laugh was lost in the loud rush of an express train overhead. They were almost home.

The hot weather lasted for ten days. Occasionally there was no sun, just a humid, grey gloom, and they expected thunder, but none came. Every day the Briggs children went under the bridge, along the rough lane and down the green road to the stream. Every evening, after paddling in the water, they went home again, tired but increasingly happy.

The task really was an enormous one, but they could at last see an improvement in the garden. Now they could walk along most of the paths. Arthur had cleared the raspberries and loganberries, and the peach trees were quite free of bindweed. The tall weeds and brambles in the flower beds were being tackled, and some daisies, scabious and golden rod were free. Megan, deserting the dandelions, had worked on the herb garden, revealing marjoram, mint, sage and other sweet-smelling things. Her neat small fingers moved unerringly to save all she could.

Mr Pelverden worked on the roof in the mornings, but

usually joined them in the afternoons. The roof was finished on the eighth day, and now the house would be safe from a downpour. At least it would be when all the broken windows were replaced. As the threat of thunder grew, he decided that new glass was his most pressing job, and it was all done only just in time.

The air took on a thick, golden quality, with dark clouds in the distance. There wasn't a breath of wind, and sounds carried a long way. Cows lowing a mile away seemed near.

On that Saturday afternoon, just before they went home, they took a tour of inspection through the house, to see the new windows. Nothing else had changed, and it was an eerie place in the thundery light. Dilys and Brian found themselves together in a dark passage.

Neither Dilys nor Arthur had made much progress with Brian, but at least he didn't avoid them so pointedly.

'I'm loving it!' she said impulsively. 'And we *are* getting on. Don't you think so, Brian?'

'I suppose so,' he agreed.

'And if it's going to rain we can start on the house. Arthur's dying to clear the attics and see if there's any treasure.'

'Treasure?' Brian seemed surprised.

'You know . . . antiques. Things people collect. Nice things for the house, or something to sell and make money.'

'I shouldn't think there's anything,' said Brian. But he sounded interested; not unfriendly, as he had done for so long.

They came out into the gloomy, littered kitchen, and found Mr Pelverden, Arthur and the little ones waiting for them.

'You get home,' Mr Pelverden said. 'Arthur says you don't like thunder, Dilys. Not that I think it'll come for hours.'

Mr Pelverden walked with them toward the garden door. He was cocking his head and frowning. There was a good deal of unpleasant noise . . . shouts, screams and raucous voices.

'I'm afraid it's one of those gangs from Manchester,' Mr Pelverden said quietly. 'Just follow me, and don't make a sound. They're down by the mill, I think. This is the kind of gang that was starting to break up the house. There have only been two lots of trouble since we came, but it's alarming. There's not much one can do against half a dozen great lads out for mischief and trouble. And we aren't on the telephone.'

Perhaps the thundery atmosphere made it worse, for Megan was not the only one who was scared. Dilys and Arthur exchanged glances, wondering how they were going to get home.

They all stood by the front steps, facing the bridge, listening intently to the din. Then, to their vast relief (and even to Mr Pelverden's, they knew), a voice shouted:

'Come on, lads! Let's be getting back! Ee, there's going to be a right bad storm.'

The shouts and voices retreated, and after a few moments

they glimpsed through the trees five youths heading in the direction of Nether Pelverden and the main road. Motor-cycle engines started up and the gang moved off. By the jerky sounds of the engines the rough lane was not very good for motor-cycles.

'Thank goodness!' said Mr Pelverden, and wiped his brow. 'Now you get off home . . . quickly!'

The storm broke as they were washing the supper dishes. It had gone almost completely dark, and they had the lights on. The railway embankment brooded above, like a threatening wave about to engulf the house.

And then the lightning flashed, thunder came with a sudden, reverberating crash, and, within minutes, the rain was pouring down. Dilys felt that perhaps she had grown up a little since that first storm, because she didn't mind this one quite so much. She kept on thinking of the garden at Nether Pelverden Manor, and how the rain would help the flowers, *if* it wasn't so heavy that it damaged them. The house was safe, anyway, with the roof whole and the windows in place. The manor house was all that mattered at the moment. And Brian.

'I think Brian is starting to melt a bit,' she said to Arthur later. She was standing by his bedroom window, wearing her pyjamas and dressing gown, watching the rain bouncing off the embankment.

'So do I,' Arthur agreed. During the long, hot days in the garden he had often tried to talk to Brian, often deliberately worked near him. Brian wouldn't talk about school, but he had not seemed to mind listening to stories about their old home in Shropshire.

Arthur admired the way Brian had kept on working, because it was clear that he did not find everything easy. Alerted by private remarks made by Dilys, Arthur had seen how Brian's hands told him things his eyes were not sure about. He had noticed on one occasion Brian unable to find his clippers, though they were lying quite near him.

Brian might be only partially sighted, but he was strong and he concentrated. And his looks had improved during the days in the garden. He no longer looked so hunched, and he was not a bad looking boy now that he was sun-tanned. Except for the awful thick glasses, of course.

Not anyone to laugh at. Arthur agreed with Dilys that the boys and girls at school wanted their heads examining. Brian had character and brains, and a very beautiful speaking voice. Once he had surprised Arthur by quoting a few lines of poetry from *A Shropshire Lad*.

The storm was over by eleven o'clock, but the rain fell all night. On Sunday morning it was still raining steadily. The air was grey and still, and the cooling towers had disappeared in the mist.

They put on their raincoats and went to the manor, eager for different work. They all decided to start on the big main kitchen, so that they could have a base for indoor work. The worst of the rubbish was carried into the store room near the back door, ready for transporation into the field.

'It will be the start of our celebration bonfire!' Dilys cried, struggling with a pile of dirty sacks. Yet her heart quailed, for the house was far worse than the garden. The bonfire was still a dream of the future.

Mr Pelverden had collected wood and coal for the day when they started on the house. But first the huge grate had to be cleared of dirt and cobwebs.

'No one would think he's a schoolmaster,' Arthur whispered, when they saw Mr Pelverden growing dirtier and dirtier.

The little ones didn't like this kind of work. They retreated to the depths of the house to play hide and seek. It was rather a scary game for only two, but Megan was brave and Melinda knew the house well enough by then for some of the 'ghosts' to have disappeared.

By lunchtime the kitchen was at least clear of the worst of the rubbish. Mr Pelverden had used a long broom to bring down the dust and cobwebs from the beams, and the floor had been swept. But the flagstones were filthy and so was the old table. After lunch, Mr Pelverden lit the fire, and at first it was dreadful. Great clouds of smoke billowed out into the room.

'What we need is a sweep!' he said, coughing. 'But Ben and I did clear the tops of the chimneys of nests and suchlike.'

But the smoke cleared after a time, and the fire burned

up. They filled the ancient iron kettles and soon had some hot water.

'But it'll take an *ocean* of hot water to do any good here!' panted Dilys, after the contents of three kettles had made only the barest impression on the floor.

Arthur and Brian swept and Dilys followed behind with a big mop. But the dirt of ages clung to that stone floor.

Mr Pelverden poured the fourth kettleful into the old bucket they were using, and two minutes later Brian kicked it over. He had been out of the room and didn't see it in the rather dark corner. He looked mortified and cross, but Arthur said quickly: 'That's the best place for it! This old floor needs a real flooding.' And he whistled as he brushed.

Brian said nothing for a long time. How he hated making silly mistakes and drawing attention to his disability. Dilys longed to say to him: 'Anyone can kick over a bucket.'

Before she finished she intended to teach Brian to say: 'Sorry! Afraid I didn't see it.' Then forget it.

By the end of the afternoon they were all filthy, but the flags were starting to come up much whiter. Dilys had even made a start on the table and the little ones came to help her to scrub. As they worked they all sang.

'You really are a wonderful crowd!' said Mr Pelverden, as they went to the cottage for a wash. 'I don't know how I'll ever thank you for all this hard work.'

He didn't need to thank them. The camaraderie and feeling of purpose were sufficient reward. Arthur and Dilys often wondered what the holidays would have been like without the task of saving Nether Pelverden Manor.

It rained off and on for another week. Occasionally the sun came out and they all rushed out into the garden. The weeds and long grass came up more easily from the soaked soil, but it was messy work, and when they went home their mother sometimes said: 'If I had a good old fashioned pump I'd put you all under it!' But she was delighted that they were so happily occupied and never complained of being lonely.

During the rainy spells they made progress in the house.

There was now a considerable pile of boxes, sacks and miscellaneous rubbish in the field, and they added to it all the time. But it was slow work clearing the kitchen passages, the store rooms and the hall. Finally they got into the dining room and the great drawing room. First the cobwebs and dust had to be removed, then Dilys intended to oil the panelling. She started to polish the long table one dreary afternoon, when, in spite of the flowers in the garden and the heavy leafage, summer seemed to have deserted them.

She was polishing and singing, helped by Megan and Melinda. Their heads were all bent over the table when there was a sudden crash. A stone whistled past, only a couple of feet from Megan. Megan screamed and covered her face as glass tinkled on to the floor by the middle window.

Dilys, shocked, looked out and saw two figures on the bridge. They were laughing and the boy's hand held another stone.

'Dan and Edith!' she cried. 'You keep down, Mellie and Meg. I'll fix *them*!'

The Briggses had not seen Dan and Edith since they started to work at the manor weeks ago. But there they were, large as life, having braved Mr Lowe.

By great good luck the heavy front door was unbolted. Mr Pelverden had been working on the hinges and getting the rust off the ancient bolts. He had gone away for the moment, but Dilys acted quickly. She took the Browns utterly by surprise by flinging open the door and rushing down the steps. She saw their astonished faces.

Dan turned and ran, but Edith just stood gaping with surprise and alarm. Dilys pounced on her fiercely and dragged her by one arm up the steps and into the hall. She kicked the door shut behind her, and it made such an ominous clang that Edith felt she was in a fortress.

Dilys hauled Edith into the dining room and said to Mellie:

'Go and tell your dad that I've taken someone prisoner. He'll have a fit when he sees that window.'

Melinda obeyed.

Edith began to cry and couldn't find a handkerchief. She looked a pathetic object as she sniffed and sobbed, but Megan eyed her without pity.

'That was wicked!' she said. 'We've worked so hard, and glass costs money. An' you might have killed me.'

'Megan's right,' said Dilys. 'And Mr Pelverden will be furious with you.'

'Let me go!' Edith wailed. '*Please!* We didn't know anyone was here. We couldn't see into the room. We were just having some fun.'

'I'll give you fun!' Dilys retorted, so fiercely that Edith sobbed anew.

'Dan's gone,' she cried. 'He's always an awful coward. He's left me.'

Chapter Eight

Two more helpers

Dilys glanced through the windows and saw Dan peering doubtfully through the wet leaves beyond the bridge.

'He hasn't run far,' she said. At that moment Arthur and Brian came in. They had been working in the drawing room.

'What's going on?' Arthur asked, staring at Edith.

Dilys explained. Edith stopped sobbing and stared at Brian.

'What's Owl doing here?' she demanded suddenly.

That infuriated Dilys even more.

'If you call people by rude names,' she said sharply, 'you'll be in a lot more trouble. We have plenty of lovely dark store rooms here. We could lock you up for a week. This house belongs to Brian's father, and we're helping to save it.' As she spoke an idea was forming in her mind. They needed more help, and Dan and Edith needed something to do. Dan and Edith might realise the stupidity of breaking windows if they did a real job for a change.

Melinda was taking a long time to find her father. Dilys said to Arthur and Brian: 'Keep an eye on her!' Then she went back to the front door. She opened it and looked out. Dan's head bobbed back into the leaves.

'You come on out, Dan Brown!' she shouted. 'Come and see what we're doing to Edith. If you don't, I'll tell the whole school you're a coward.'

Maybe Dan didn't think much of that threat, but he was curious. He had no idea what was going on, but it seemed to be interesting. He advanced slowly over the bridge. His shabby raincoat dripped water into the tops of his boots, and his face was red, wet and shining.

'What you done to Edith?' he demanded.

'Come and see,' Dilys invited and held the great door wide. Dan shrugged and stepped over the threshold. And at that moment Mr Pelverden came from the back of the house. Melinda was clinging to his hand.

They all went into the dining room. At first Mr Pelverden ignored Dan and Edith. He walked over to the window and eyed the damage gloomily. He had had an awful job fitting the glass into the stone mullions. Then he looked at the table smeared with furniture polish, the dusters abandoned. His eyes lighted on the large stone on the floor. And he came over all schoolmaster, so that Dan cringed and Edith sniffled again.

'And who are you, may I ask? *Local* hooligans, I suppose. Where do you live? I want an answer this very moment.'

Dan wasn't wholly a coward, though the stern man was very intimidating. They seemed to be in something strange

84

and difficult, but it *was* interesting. And somehow the presence of the Briggs children, so much at home in the house, reassured him.

'Dan and Edith Brown, Sir. And our dad works for Colonel Melling. We haven't a mother. If you complain to our dad he'll beat me. Not Edith. She's only a girl.'

'Girls, in my experience, are quite as good as boys,' Mr Pelverden said crisply. 'Or as bad. Maybe Edith could do with a beating, too.'

'But we're sorry. We thought the old place was empty. Though we *did* wonder why there were new windows, and all the weeds gone.'

'So you promptly set out to break the windows again?'
But Mr Pelverden had caught Dilys's eye, and he saw she
was trying to convey some message. No mother . . . and he
had heard a good deal about Colonel Melling. How he
wouldn't have children around the farm.

'They go to our school, Dad,' said Brian, speaking for
the first time.

'They do? Poor school!' said Mr Pelverden scathingly.

Dilys wished she could get Mr Pelverden alone, but it
wasn't possible. She said: 'I've been thinking. Trouble with
Dan and Edith is that they haven't anything to do. I
thought perhaps they could come and help.'

Arthur laughed. 'Help? Them?'

Brian made a small sound of protest, and Dilys looked at
him. Brian wouldn't like it, but it wouldn't hurt Dan and
Edith to get to know him better before the autumn term.
It wouldn't really hurt Brian, either, perhaps.

'They'd be two more pairs of hands,' she said simply.

'You have a point there,' said Mr Pelverden. 'But how
do we know they'd like to help? And their father might
object.'

'Dad would be glad to get rid of us, and so would our
aunt,' said Edith. The holidays had been so lonely and
boring. Something was going on in the old manor house,
and even Mr Pelverden's presence would be better than
more days with nothing to do. They had often wondered
where the Briggs children had gone.

'They'd make a mess of it, Dad,' Brian protested. 'I bet

they don't know weeds from flowers. They'd only . . .'

'We *do* know weeds from flowers,' Dan insisted. 'Honest. We had a lovely little garden when Mum was alive. She let us help her. Auntie hasn't the time, and we . . . we gave it up.'

He hadn't meant to sound pathetic, but Mr Pelverden was won over. They weren't really hooligans, and the more children around the place the better for Brian.

He was delighted with the way his son had grown more easy and friendly. It was taking some time, but Brian was improving all the while. Though it was clear that he didn't like Dan and Edith.

Quickly Mr Pelverden outlined the story of Nether Pelverden Manor, and how they were trying to improve it before men came to look it over and perhaps give a grant for its preservation.

Dan and Edith were not the kind to feel it was a romantic task, but they were interested. And both looked more enthusiastic when Arthur said: 'When it's all done, *if* it ever is, we're going to have a huge bonfire and fireworks to celebrate. As well as a banquet in this room, at this very table. So you'd better get moving and help to polish it.'

'I seemed blessed with endless free labour,' Mr Pelverden murmured. 'Sometimes I wonder if I ought to accept it.' But they didn't hear him. Already Dan and Edith were taking off their wet raincoats and asking for more dusters.

'All come and have some lemonade and cake at the

cottage in half an hour,' said Mr Pelverden. 'A word with you, Dilys.'

Dilys followed him into the hall. They stood close under the staircase and he spoke in a low voice. 'Was that what you wanted? Those two . . .'

Dilys nodded. She had got to know Mr Pelverden well during the weeks of hard work, singing and laughter.

'Yes. I was mad with them at first. They can be awful. But . . . Well, they're not so bad, really. Only . . . thoughtless.'

'Brian doesn't like them. Why?'

'Because . . . Well, they've been stupid, like the others. They call him names like Owl and Four Eyes, and laugh when he can't see things.'

'I see.' His face clouded. He suffered always for his son's humiliation. 'Then . . .'

'I'm going to talk to them,' she said. 'And I thought it'd help if they get to know Brian better.'

'All right,' he said abruptly. 'I leave it to you.'

Dilys stared after him. He often made her feel quite old, as if she were grown up and really sensible. It was a nice feeling.

She found Arthur by her side. He was frowning and looked cross.

'You are an idiot, Dilly! Why'd you wish that pair on us?'

'I'm not an idiot,' she answered, and hoped it was true, that it would all work out. 'We'll make them work.

Think how fast we'll get on with another two to help.'

Arthur grunted. 'I'll believe it when we see what they do.'

Dan and Edith were waiting at the gate of Flash Cottage the next morning when the Briggs children came out. Dan carried their picnic lunch in a haversack, and they both had forks and hoes, though it was drizzling.

The Browns actually looked shy and subdued, but by the time they all reached the green lane they were talking in quite a friendly fashion.

'It's nice to have somewhere to go,' Edith said, as they reached the mill.

'It's fun,' said Dilys. 'You'll like it.'

It was now part of life to emerge from the trees and see the manor house before them. The bridge was quite free of dandelions and grass, thanks to the work of the little ones, and the red sandstone steps rose cleanly to the front door. The moat was still pale green, but Mr Pelverden said he had written somewhere for advice. He hoped to find something that would remove the slime and water weeds.

'Our house is beautiful,' said Megan.

'It isn't our house,' said Arthur, but it *felt* like their own place. For they were trying to make it safe, and it certainly was beautiful.

'Mr Pelverden is going to try to remove that awful "D",' Dilys couldn't resist saying, staring at the front door. Dan blushed fierily and looked ashamed.

89

Dan and Edith did work. It was still too wet for the garden, so they started on the panelling in the dining room. Brian didn't work with them, but went on polishing the floor in the drawing room. Sometimes Arthur joined him for a while.

The only exciting episode of that day was when Dan found an old wooden tray in a cupboard in the panelling. Before anyone could stop him, he had taken it to the top of the first flight of stairs and was tobogganing down.

The descent of the tray made an awful noise, and Dan's shriek as he and the tray parted before they reached the bottom awoke the echoes all over the house.

'You are an idiot!' Dilys stormed. 'What do you think this is? The Cresta run?' They had seen a Swiss film on television.

Dan picked himself up, looking sheepish. He had hurt his leg, but was too proud to admit it.

'You might have broken your neck,' said Brian. He and Arthur had emerged from the dining room.

'Oh, shut up, Four—' Then Dan stopped. Dilys had had a few words to say on the way home the day before. 'I couldn't resist it,' he ended lamely.

Dilys seized the tray, which was elaborately carved, though covered with dirt. 'This belongs to the house. I'll clean it,' she said. 'It's nice.'

Before the sun shone again hotly, they had cleaned the main bedrooms and were able, at last, to start on the attics. The attics had attracted Arthur since the very beginning, but he had resisted them, knowing there was more important work to be done first.

The fact that the roof was repaired had kept out the recent rain, but damp and decay had done their worst. The whole top floor was in a dreadful state, thick with mildew and dust, and with spiders' webs and abandoned birds' nests.

On the first session Arthur plunged in triumphantly and began dragging boxes out of corners. There was a sudden grinding noise and he shouted with alarm as one leg disappeared through the floor boards. Dilys, Dan and Edith rushed to the rescue.

'I've gone through to the ceiling!' Arthur gasped.

But he hadn't. There was space between the floor boards and the beams and plaster below.

Mr Pelverden, hearing the rumpus, came to see what was happening.

'I hope it isn't dry rot,' he said gloomily. 'All these boards are rotten and will have to be replaced. I must get some good wood. Be very careful, all of you. Move cautiously up here.'

They carried out an enormous amount of useless rubbish. It was a terrible task getting it downstairs and into the field. But there *was* some treasure. They amassed what seemed interesting, or even valuable, in one of the big bedrooms below. There was a child's rocking horse that delighted Megan and Melinda. When cleaned it was really splendid, and still rocked. There was an old screen, worn and shabby, but beautifully carved. In a wooden box pushed to the back of a shelf they found, carefully wrapped in rotting black velvet, a set of silver forks and spoons.

Mr and Mrs Pelverden were really thrilled with that find. They were even more delighted when a very large box was found behind some moth-filled armchairs in another attic. For it contained a wonderful dinner service, white and grey, edged with gold.

'This is really valuable,' Mr Pelverden said. He carefully lifted out plates of different sizes and the lid of an enormous vegetable dish.

'I don't know who'd use it these days,' said his wife.

'You could sell it and make money for the house,' Arthur suggested. This was his find.

'Well, we'll wait,' Mr Pelverden said slowly. '*If* we get a grant we'll have to show the house to the public sometimes. We could try and make the dining room look the way it did long ago. Put all this out on the table, with the silver. Grandfather must have forgotten about this stuff. Maybe he couldn't get up the attic stairs. If he'd remembered I expect it would have been sold.'

There was a box full of old Victorian toys, which Mr Pelverden said were probably valuable now. But he let Megan and Melinda empty the box and dust everything carefully.

The last real treasure was found in a battered trunk with iron bands. All the children crowded around as it was dragged out into the middle of the attic.

'There will be a skeleton in there,' said Megan.

'There *won't*!' said Edith, but she backed away.

The trunk was not locked, but Mr Pelverden had trouble getting the lid up. Mrs Pelverden, who was fascinated by these things that belonged to the house, went for a thin iron bar. The lid shot up, and they waited for moths to fly out, but nothing happened. Only a faint, ghostly smell of long ago moth balls came to their nostrils.

In the trunk was household linen. Enormous white tablecloths with wonderful embroidery, linen table napkins, delicate lace antimacassars.

They carried one tablecloth down to the dining room,

and, each holding it a few feet apart, spread it over the long table. Clearly it belonged there.

Even the imaginations of Dan and Edith had begun to work during the long days at Nether Pelverden Manor. They stood in awe as the great cloth slid into place.

'We could use it for the banquet,' said Edith.

'Do you know,' said Mrs Pelverden, 'I think we will. If that banquet ever comes off.'

'Oh, it will. It must,' cried Dilys.

For the summer holidays were passing. In a week it would be September. In two weeks they would go back to school.

'There's still so much to do,' said Arthur. 'Particularly in the garden.'

The August weather had often been dreadful, but the weather forecasts were better. There was hope of a prolonged dry spell.

'I've written to the Society for the Preservation of Old Houses,' said Mr Pelverden. 'And I've said the house will be ready for them to see in a couple of weeks. And I sent the photographs.' For one thing he had done was to take a complete record, showing the house as it was when he took it over, and then the gradual improvements. They had all grown used to his flash bulbs going off as they worked.

'What shall we do if they won't help?' Brian asked.

'We'll cross that bridge when we come to it,' said his father.

Chapter Nine

Dilys and Brian

The fine weather came next day and they all moved into the garden. The lily pond was clear and Mr Pelverden filled it with water. Edith, surprisingly, arrived next morning carrying a bowl of goldfish. They were awkward to transport, but she managed it without many splashes.

'No water lilies this year,' she said. 'But you can have our fish. They'll like the new pool.' Edith was a different girl now, though she and Dan still quarrelled with each other.

'That's very nice of you, Edith,' said Mr Pelverden.

They spread out all over the garden. Arthur began to dig the corner reserved for vegetables. The little ones were in the one-time asparagus bed, trying to clear what was left of long grass and weeds. Dilys was struggling with the weeds around the biggest clump of golden rod. The flowers were just about to open. There was something very autumnal about golden rod. It made her feel sad.

Brian worked not far away. He was hoeing around the roses. Though they had been choked for so long, they had flowered and were still flowering. Every so often he and

Dilys talked. They were friends now, in a kind of way.

Then Dilys forgot and left her hoe across the path. Brian, moving away from the roses, promptly tripped over it. Dilys went hot all over . . . even hotter than she had been before in the strong sun.

'I'm sorry, Brian,' she said.

Brian's face was inscrutable as he picked himself up.

'Clumsy me!' he said, in a tight voice.

And so it was time to make him talk . . . to make him see how wrong he was not to explain.

Dilys was scared. Brian's was a strong personality, and in a way she was in awe of him. But she faced him bravely.

'It was my fault. I know you can't see very well.'

The words 'I know you can't see very well' seemed to hang in the sweet-scented, sunlit air of the walled garden. Brian stared at her through his thick glasses. His face was hard.

The sunlight shimmered on the roses, the phlox and the opening golden rod. The heat seemed to come in waves from the old, enclosing walls. A ripe peach seemed as big as a melon as Dilys blinked. The sounds of laughter and voices might have been a mile away.

Brian said nothing, and he didn't move. Dilys wasn't very old, but she had unusual wisdom, as Mr Pelverden had found out. Her eyes cleared and she looked at the garden, seeing it in every delicate detail. How did Brian see it? As a golden blur, maybe. He could not appreciate the beauty of each petal, each leaf, the tracery on a butterfly's wings.

Dilys thought of being quite blind, but Brian's father had said his eyes might go no worse. Still, it was awful that he should always have to miss the fine lines, the beauty of little flowers in the grass. For him, it might be even worse that he so often made a fool of himself because of his disability.

But now was the moment. She had known somewhere in her mind all through the long holidays that it *would* come. Brian had to go back to school. Dan and Edith had learned to understand, but the others wouldn't learn so quickly.

She gulped. They were alone in their hot patch of garden.

'Brian . . .' Her voice sounded thin and small. 'Look, listen to me. We're friends, aren't we? I know you hate to talk about your eyes . . .'

Brian spoke then. 'I *can't* talk about them,' he said.

'But you'll have to. It would make everything ten times easier. It isn't anything to be ashamed of.'

'Oh, isn't it?' Brian asked fiercely.

'No, of course it isn't. It's not your fault. Just . . . Just one of those things that happen. Think how it must be for *anyone* who has something wrong with them. You're good-looking and clever. You aren't deformed or anything like that. So please . . .'

'You don't understand,' Brian said. 'I wake up every morning and *know* I'll be the same. I wake up in the night and switch on the light, to make sure I haven't gone blind.

Being the same is better than that. But I do silly things, and it kills me every time.'

'Yes. Yes, I *know*,' she said impatiently. 'I've seen. I do understand. But you're an idiot. You can't alter it, can you? So you ought to deal with it in a different way.'

'The others all laugh at me. Dan and Edith don't now . . .'

'Dan and Edith have learned sense, working here. They know you're far cleverer than they are. Brian, when . . . when you do anything, do please just say: "I couldn't see that". If you drop something and can't find it, or do the wrong thing, just *say* it. I know it's awful, not being able to see, but it just is so. Even the teachers forget you can't, because you're so grimly proud.'

'I'm not!' His voice was sharp.

'Yes, you are. You hate having something wrong with you. So should I. But you might have no legs. That would be worse.'

'Would it?'

Dilys supposed it would be. Yet if you had no legs that was that. The remark about turning on the light during the night had struck fear into her own heart.

'Anyway,' she said quietly, 'you're talking about it now. Do it to me, and maybe you'll get used to it.'

'You're not like any of the others,' Brian muttered.

'Well, I liked you from the first. I expect it made me understand. So don't be a fool. *Say* it. It'll help.'

'I'll try,' he said, and went back to the roses.

At least he didn't seem to hate her for what she had just said. And just possibly he might be able to make the real, brave effort to explain casually that he couldn't see very well. It *would* be brave. Dilys understood that.

She told Arthur about it on the way home. Dan and Edith were ahead with Megan. Arthur listened interestedly.

'Brian wouldn't have taken that from me,' he said. 'I did try once, when he dropped a screw right at his feet and couldn't see it. But he closed up like a clam and didn't speak for the rest of the afternoon. I hope it works, that's all. He has ten times more character than Dan and Edith and most of the others at school.'

'But you like Dan now?'

'Oh, Dan's all right. Isn't he good at any kind of woodwork? He helped Mr Pelverden really well with those floorboards. And he's making a little stool for Megan.'

Dilys stopped and stretched, flinging her arms wide and arching her back. The lane was filled with hot late afternoon sunlight.

'I wish these holidays need never end,' she said.

The next day was Sunday, and there were people down by the stream all afternoon. Everywhere had been quiet for a long time, because of the rain and cold, so they were at first alarmed when they heard laughter and voices. Arthur went to investigate once or twice, and he reported that it was just ordinary people. Not one of those awful gangs.

A few of them came up to the house, and stood on the

bridge taking photographs. But they did not come any closer and soon went away again.

They worked in the garden all afternoon, except for Mr and Mrs Pelverden, who were in the house. Mr Pelverden was painting the old beams in the kitchen to preserve them, and Mrs Pelverden had the horrible job of cleaning the old electric stove. For electricians were coming on Monday to look at the wiring all over the house.

At five o'clock Dilys was working with Brian in the last wild corner. 'Time we stopped,' Brian said. At the same moment someone knocked at the garden door.

Dilys was nearest, so she went to the door and opened it. Outside, smiling apologetically, stood a tall man. He was casually dressed, with a camera over his shoulder.

'Excuse me,' he said. 'I know it's kind of rude of me, but the house is so old. I thought maybe it was empty, then I heard voices over the wall. I guess you wouldn't . . . your father wouldn't let me see over the house?'

He was American, Dilys thought, and he looked very nice. What was he doing in this remote corner of Cheshire? He seemed to read her thoughts, for he went on: 'I'm from New York City and my name is Milton Carew. I'm visiting with my daughter in Manchester. She's living there now. I've been exploring.'

Brian had joined Dilys in the doorway.

'I'll ask Dad,' he said, and went to fetch Mr Pelverden. Dilys began to explain about what they were doing, and how they hoped to save the manor house. The American was enthusiastic and beamed when Mr Pelverden appeared and said he could see the house if he liked.

Brian and Dilys followed during the tour of the house. The American looked wistfully at the old screen and at the other things they had found in the attics.

'It's a real romantic tale!' he kept on saying. And then: 'Do you want to sell any of these lovely old things?'

But Mr Pelverden shook his head firmly.

'They belong to the house,' he said. 'It may be different if we don't get a grant.'

Back in the kitchen Mr Milton Carew took out a visiting card and a cheque book.

'It was kind of you to permit me to see the house. I'll be grateful if you'll let me know what happens. This is a bit of old England, and I'll never forget it. Now please let me make a donation.'

Dilys gasped. Perhaps he was a millionaire. Mr Pelverden, looking startled, shook his head.

'It's just a house in private hands at the moment. I can't take your money, Mr Carew.'

But the American was writing busily. He tore off the cheque and laid it on the table.

'Just a little offering. Spend it on the house, *please*.'

And before Mr Pelverden had the chance to reply he had gone. He thanked them over his shoulder until he was out of sight through the garden door.

'One hundred dollars,' Dilys whispered. 'Is that a lot of money?'

'About forty pounds, I think,' said Mr Pelverden. 'I'm not sure of the rate of exchange just now. I can't use it, of course.' But his voice was wistful. Forty pounds was sorely needed, for he had used most of his savings. The electricians' bill would probably be high, and they needed plants and new rose bushes.

'I don't see why you shouldn't, Dad,' said Brian. 'He wants to feel he's helped to save a bit of old England.'

'We ought to frame it,' said Mrs Pelverden. 'Our first real visitor.'

Chapter Ten

The siege

The last days of the holidays began to fly past. They had done everything that seemed possible, yet new tasks turned up every day. For one thing the weeds grew so fast.

A letter came from the Society, and it expressed great interest in Nether Pelverden Manor. Two representatives, Mr Jones and Mr Crawford, would come and see the house on Monday, September the sixth.

'That's the day before we go back to school,' Dilys said. 'Oh, what *shall* we do if it doesn't come off?' And she went for an anxious stroll through the house. How different it was now from the way it had looked during that very first tour of inspection. But she knew, because she had often heard Mr Pelverden talk about it, that there were things that ought to be done to the fabric of the building. The staircase should be strengthened, and some of the ancient panelling repaired by experts, as well as work undertaken outside.

In the garden the golden rod stood tall and glowing, and there were clumps of dahlias and michaelmas daisies. The air was mellow and blue smoke drifted from Mr Lowe's farm. Autumn was on the way . . . the lovely summer would soon end. But *how* would it end? With rejoicing, or with failure after all their efforts?

That evening they were just approaching the gate of Flash Cottage when Mrs Briggs burst out, beckoning.

'Quick!' she called. 'Something on television!'

They raced indoors, jostling each other.

'Why, it's Mr Laurie!' Arthur gasped.

'Mr Laurie doesn't look like that,' said Megan. 'He's poor and shabby and untidy. But that's his nice voice.'

'It *is* Mr Laurie,' Mrs Briggs said. 'This is the opening of an exhibition of his work in Manchester. See all the important people? It's his *tenth* show, the announcer said. It's just incredible! He certainly looked poor, and I never thought much of Dilly's picture . . .'

Dilys had fallen on her knees in front of the set. Different pictures were being shown; ones they had seen leaning against the scanty furniture in the old cottage.

'John Z. Laurie has immortalised a certain corner of Cheshire,' said the announcer. 'He has spent the summer living by a remote flash. His own unique style has a curious vividness. He is one of Britain's present great painters.'

They had been out rowing with a great artist. They had drunk lemonade with him, and talked as if he were just an ordinary person. Dilys was breathless with the wonder of it. She had wanted him to be rich and famous, and he had been all the time.

'But I *knew* his pictures were good,' she said.

'His smallest paintings sell for several hundred pounds, and their value increases every year.'

'You can sell your picture, Dilly,' said Arthur.

'I'll never sell it!' Dilys said fiercely. And, the moment the programme changed, she went into her bedroom and stood staring at the picture over her bed.

'That I really own one!' she said to herself. 'He *gave* it to me, though he could have got a lot of money for it.'

It was so exciting and joyful a thing that, for a while, she almost forgot about that other greater thing that was pending. The fate of Nether Pelverden Manor.

On their last Saturday evening before the holidays ended, they all stayed to have supper with the Pelverdens. It was a tight squeeze to get them into the little living room, but it was managed. It was a lovely evening, golden and still, and the windows were wide open.

They had just finished the meal when Brian looked up.

'What's that awful noise?' he asked. 'I thought I heard motor bikes a while ago, and now . . .'

'It's a gang!' said Mr Pelverden, and his face went grim. The others were all silent with fear. A gang *now*, when the house waited to hear its fate. When it was to be visited by the important men on Monday morning.

'They'll probably go away again,' said Mrs Pelverden.

But the shouts and yells increased. Megan and Melinda looked really scared, and the others were secretly scared, too. When Mr Pelverden said he'd go and take a look, the older children followed him. They walked through the garden and Mr Pelverden unbolted the garden door. He always kept it locked when they were in the cottage.

'You keep back,' he ordered. The awful shouts were growing nearer. The gang was approaching the house. They emerged from the trees . . . six hefty youths, cat-calling as they came.

'Bin 'ere before, we 'ave!' shouted one. 'Broke windows. Someone's bin an' mended 'em, but the old place is still empty. Break one good an' proper, and, Sid, you give me a back. Let's get in!'

They had not seen Mr Pelverden peering cautiously around the wall of the house. He turned and signalled to the white-faced young people behind him to keep back.

'But what can we *do*?' whispered Dilys.

'Where's a stone? A right big 'un?'

'There's no stones here,' said a rough, loud voice.

No, there weren't. The whole approach to the manor had been cleared. The track was uneven with hardened mud, that was all.

'Back to the stream, lads! Find some good big 'uns!'

Mr Pelverden was a tall, strong man, and a school-master. But he knew he couldn't tackle six man-sized youths, bent on trouble. And there was still no telephone, though he had applied to have one at the cottage.

'Let's arm ourselves and rush them,' suggested Arthur.

'With what?' asked Mr Pelverden.

'Rakes and hoes and things. There are plenty.'

'Not much protection against stones,' Mr Pelverden said grimly. 'And I'm responsible for you. Your safety is more important than the house.'

'But we *can't* let them . . .'

There was no possibility of immediate help. The youths were blocking the way to Lowe's Farm, and to the main road, and all the Saturday picnickers must have gone home by then.

'We may not be able to stop them breaking windows,' said Dan, remembering, with shame, how *he* had delighted in doing the same thing, 'but if they get into the house we can attack them. Drive them back. They'll have used all the stones by the time they're in. And . . .'

'They may have knuckle-dusters or something,' said Edith.

'But they couldn't get near *us*. Not if we charge them, brandishing the weapons. They'll be scared stiff, and surprised, too. They think the house is empty,' Arthur said.

'That's true,' agreed Mr Pelverden. 'But . . .'

'We *have* to do what we can.'

'Where's the nearest telephone?' Dilys asked.

'A mile away. Up on the main road by the bus stop.'

'Isn't there another way we can get out? Over the field where the bonfire stuff is, and through the wire fence? That'd bring us out where they can't see us. Dial nine-nine-nine, and there may be a police car somewhere near.'

'I'll go,' said Brian.

They all looked at him. He was very pale.

'They *might* see you,' said Dilys. 'They could have gone up the lane a bit, looking for really big stones.'

'I'll risk it. Someone has to go.'

Yes, someone had to. Though a lot of damage could be

done in the time it would take to get to the telephone and for help to come.

And then Brian threw up his head. The lowering sun glinted on his thick glasses. He said quietly, looking at his father: 'I wouldn't be much good brandishing a rake. I might hit the wrong person. But I can see well enough to get out of here and escape them. I'll ring the police quick as I can.'

There was a moment's silence. There were still shouts and raucous laughter in the distance. Mr Pelverden looked at his son, and Dilys held her breath. Brian had done it. In this moment of terrible anxiety, he had been brave and spoken about his sight.

'Yes, go, lad,' said Mr Pelverden. 'But be careful getting through the fence. We'll do what we can here.'

They ran back to tell Mrs Pelverden and the little ones what was happening. Mrs Pelverden protested, but they armed themselves with garden implements and entered the manor by the back door. The nearing shouts had told them that the boys were coming back.

It was very dark in the passages, but the hall was lighter, for all the doors were open into the various rooms. A crash of breaking glass told them that the attack had started. Mr Pelverden blocked the way into the drawing room with his hoe.

'Wait!' he hissed.

'But the *windows*!'

'I'll fix them tomorrow. I have some glass left. Keep

away from the stones. I don't want anyone to get hit.'

It took several stones for the youths to make what they thought was a satisfactory gap. But then there was comparative silence, broken only by rough-voiced argument. The sandstone base was high. Sid's back was evidently not sufficient to help anyone to get up, knock out the rest of the glass and enter.

'We could rush them *now*,' breathed Dan.

'No,' said Mr. Pelverden. 'Some of them may still have stones. Let one or two of them get in.' He hated violence of any kind. He deeply disliked involving the young people in this affair. But the drawing-room door did not lock on the outside. If they once overran the house, the youths might do bad damage.

They were all thinking about Brian. After a quarter of a mile the surface of the lane was quite good and he might make fast progress. Say twenty minutes to allow him to get there and make the call. It would depend if there was a police car in the vicinity, then it had to get down the lane as far as it could. Ten minutes, at least, had passed.

They all waited in the hall. Dilys could hear Edith's heavy breathing. 'After all our work!' she was muttering to herself. It seemed strange that Dan and Edith, who had started so badly, should now be up against the kind of vandalism to which they might have aspired when they were older, if they had not learned to work for a reason.

Someone called Bill seemed to have managed to get within reach of the window. They heard more glass tinkling into the room. Evidently Bill was clearing the dangerous edges.

'Chuck up your leather jacket, Ed!' he shouted. 'Don't want me to bleed to death climbing in, do you?'

'Me good jacket'll get spoilt by the sharp edges!'

'Want to get in, don't you? Better your jacket than us. So shurrup and chuck it up here.'

But Bill seemed to be having a struggle to get himself through the comparatively small space. The windows were all divided into sections, being mullioned.

'Couldn't we stop them *before* . . .?' Dilys whispered.

'If we do,' Mr Pelverden whispered back, 'they'll turn really nasty and break half the windows in the house. The longer this takes the better. Brian may have reached the 'phone.'

Then there was a thud and a squeal. Bill was in the room.

'Rotten tiny windows!' he complained. 'But 'ere I am. King of the Castle! Come on, lads! One by one . . . quick! There's nowt in this room. Let's go and explore.'

'Give us a hand, then!'

After three minutes or so there was another thud. But it had dawned on the two boys making backs outside that they weren't going to make it into the house.

'Go an' open the front door!' called one, brighter than the rest. 'Use your loaf, Bill!'

Bill rushed across the drawing room, followed by his companion. At the door, to his utter stupefaction, his way was barred by a menacing line of rakes and hoes.

'Cor!' he gasped, and stepped back, his heavy boots landing on the other boy's feet. The second youth lost his balance and they fell in a heap, shouting with fury and fear.

'What's all this?' Bill cried, struggling to get up.

'Take one step out of that room and you'll know,' said Mr Pelverden, in his loudest and sternest voice.

There wasn't even the need for a charge of rakes and hoes. Bill scrambled over his still prone companion and made for the window. He tried to throw himself out headlong and stuck.

'Get up, Ed!' he yelled. 'Give us a push!'

Ed, not knowing *who* was manning the weapons outside the door, for they had all kept out of sight, was almost crying with fear. Bill's urging turned to groans of terror. 'If I go out on me head I'll break me neck!'

He was a big chap, and though he had been able to get through the window when he had his wits more or less about him, he now seemed hopelessly stuck. Outside, his puzzled friends were yelling questions, and, inside, Ed was practically having hysterics. Trapped, he roared and wailed: 'Let me out! There's an army or summat in here. Or *ghosts.*'

Terror had changed to amusement among the party in the hall. It was now farcical, and Dilys and Edith had the giggles. But they still held their weapons at the ready across the door.

And then, long before they had dared to hope, they heard the distant sound of police sirens, coming nearer.

The ones outside heard the sound, too, and fled. Bill shouted and fell back into the room, and Ed, almost trampling on him, took his place at the window. Mr Pelverden and the others were now in the doorway, watching. Ed shot out and down and landed painfully on the cleared cobblestones below the sandstone base. Bill, at bay, faced his captors.

'Just keep quite still,' said Mr Pelverden.

Bill didn't obey. He tried again for the window, and, after a few agonising struggles, shot through. Shouting in desperation, he went after his companions.

But the police car was in time. It had drawn up behind the parked motor-cycles, blocking the lane. And two policemen, with Brian hovering behind, met the fleeing, scared boys head on. There was no fight left in them, and they capitulated meekly. They gave their names and addresses, and the numbers of their motor-cycles were also taken.

When the explanations were over, Mr Pelverden walked home with the Briggses and the Browns. Megan was very indignant because she had missed most of the excitement.

'I could have a held a hoe, too,' she said.

'We got off with only two windows broken,' Mr Pelverden said thankfully. 'I'll mend them in the morning.'

Chapter Eleven

Back to school

Tension was high on Monday morning. Both Arthur and Dilys had had wakeful nights, for they were both haunted by the fear that all their work would have been for nothing.

'I was sure it would pour with rain,' Dilys said. 'But at least it's simply beautiful. No wind and hot already.'

Mr Pelverden had said they could be there, because he wanted to introduce all his helpers to the visitors. But he insisted that they must keep well out of the way at first and be very quiet. So Melinda and Megan went off to play ball at the far end of the field, and the older ones sat in the yard outside the cottage. They were uneasy and restless.

Mr Jones and Mr Crawford were expected at ten-thirty, and Mr Pelverden was waiting up at the house to admit them through the front door. Mrs Pelverden took pity on the anxious group in the yard and asked them to help her. Edith and Dilys could peel potatoes, and the boys could shell peas and scrape carrots. They agreed eagerly, because they were glad to have something to do. But their ears were cocked for the sound of voices in the garden.

It was a full hour before Brian, who had the keenest

hearing, cried: 'They're just coming into the garden!' And Arthur and Dan sprang up to peer through the door.

The three men were at the top end of the walled garden. The strangers were middle-aged men, dressed in city clothes. Their voices were loud and clear, and Arthur returned to say: 'They think it's a charming old garden. And it's a miracle we've done so much in a few weeks. Of course they've seen the pictures of what it used to be like.'

It was another twenty minutes before the men came into the yard, and by then all the children were lined up. Their hair was combed and their hands washed. Mrs Pelverden hovered in the background, ready to take the visitors into the living room for coffee and home made cake.

'So these are your helpers?' Both men solemnly shook hands with each of them.

'We did work *awfully* hard,' said Megan, not at all shy.

They then had to wait again, until the adults emerged. Mr Jones was saying: 'Well, I think there's an excellent chance that the house will be scheduled as worth preserving. But of course the matter will have to go before the Board. It will be about three weeks before you hear anything definite, I'm afraid.'

Three more weeks of awful suspense!

But they all had plenty to think about, for the next morning found the three Briggs children setting off to catch the school bus. The reformed Dan and Edith were waiting at their own gate, and not still eating their breakfast, either.

It was strange to climb into the already crowded bus. It seemed so long since they were first called the flash children. Dilys held Megan on her knee and thought over the weeks since they had come to that countryside. Already even the long days in the walled garden seemed like a dream. Brian . . . How would Brian be at school?

Mr Pelverden had just dropped Brian and Melinda at the school gates as the bus drew up. Dilys pushed her way out quickly and joined Brian. As they went into school together, she was alarmed to find her friend very quiet. But he no longer hunched his shoulders so much. He was very sun-tanned and he had grown taller during the weeks of hard work.

Dan and Edith being his friends made a difference, and the first time someone addressed Brian as 'Owl' Dan said: 'You shut up! It's rude to call people names.'

Somehow Brian seemed a person to be respected. He still, of course, did the same awkward things because he couldn't see. But he had learned his hard lesson, and after he had said once or twice: 'I can't see very well, you know,' his behaviour came to be understood much better. Dilys once heard one of the boys say to another: 'I never knew he couldn't see properly. I just thought he was a bit of a fool.'

'*You* were the fool,' said Dilys. 'You might have guessed.'

But, behind all the doings of school, was anxiety over the fate of the house. And finally came the news that all was well. Everyone was wild with joy, and Mr Pelverden immediately made plans for further repairs.

'Now we can have the banquet!' cried Melinda.

So there came a Saturday evening in early October when they all went to the manor. Mr and Mrs Briggs were invited, and they drove around by road. It meant taking a detour of several miles, but it would be dark when they came home and then the car would be welcome. Mr and Miss Brown were invited, too, and they also went by car, with Dan and Edith sitting excitedly in the back. It was a lovely soft evening, with a full moon rising over the flat countryside.

When they arrived there were two surprise visitors, Mr John Z. Laurie and a tall, handsome woman, whom he introduced as his wife. They all wondered why they were there, but Brian, who seemed to be in the secret, wouldn't explain.

Though it was not yet wholly dark the manor house blazed with lights, and Dilys and Edith gasped with incredulous joy when they were all led into the dining room. One of the wonderful old cloths had been carefully laundered and covered the very long table. On the table flickered candles in silver holders, and there were bowls of autumn flowers from the garden. The silver spoons and forks, and the beautiful old dinner service, were in use, too.

'It really is a banquet,' Megan whispered, in awe.

'A very simple meal, really,' said Mrs Pelverden. 'But it's been cooked in the manor kitchen.' And she and two

helpers she had found in Snaith carried in the soup.

The house, of course, was still almost unfurnished, and the chairs around the great table were a mixed assortment. But no one bothered about that. At first all the young people were shy and quiet, and Dilys was lost in dreams because it all seemed so miraculous. As the shadows deepened beyond the mullioned windows, she looked out across the moat.

'I can hardly believe it,' she whispered to Brian.

Mr Laurie was very jolly and made jokes. So they didn't feel in awe of him for long because he was a famous artist. Finally, when they had finished their coffee and delicious little sugar biscuits, Mr Pelverden rose to his feet.

'I want to thank you all,' he said. 'You were all splendid,

and, because of you, Nether Pelverden Manor may be here for a few hundred years more.'

'Shall you all live here now?' Megan asked.

'I'm afraid not. Even with the grant we couldn't really afford to do that, and we are very comfortable in the cottage. But I have news for you. Mr Laurie has agreed to rent the house for at least a year. Mrs Laurie, and their son and daughter will be coming to live here in two or three months' time. The Society prefers to know the house is occupied, and the Lauries are willing to open it to the public occasionally.'

'Oh, how wonderful!' Dilys cried. 'I'm so glad! So we'll be able to see your pictures, Mr Laurie.'

'I'm going to make one of the attics into a studio,'

the artist explained. 'One with a good North light.'

'And now for the bonfire!' said Mr Pelverden.

As the flames leaped up into the moonlight, the men began to let off fireworks. Dilys stood near Brian.

'I'm so glad that we became the flash children,' she said softly, watching a rocket soaring into the sky. 'Shropshire was lovely, but we belong here now. And we'll always help to keep the garden beautiful.'

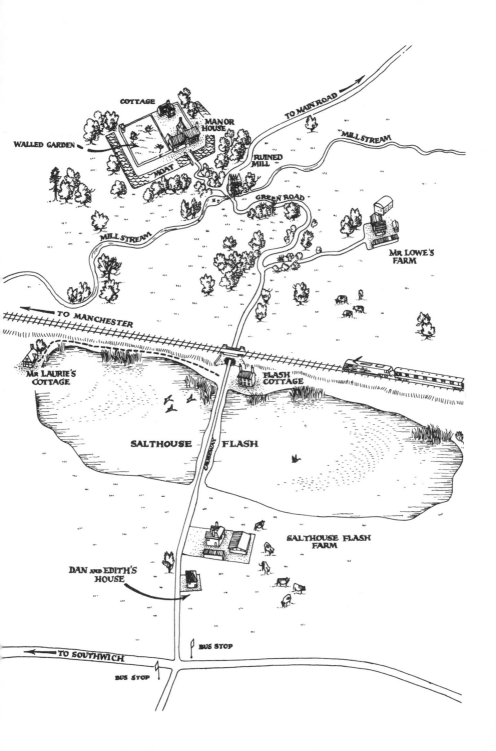